SABLE POINT MURDER

JILL QUINT , MD FORENSIC PATHOLOGIST

ALEC PECHE

ACKNOWLEDGMENTS

Thanks to my first reader, GM Meyer. She called this story her favorite after grammar and timeline corrections.

I also want to thank my editor, Ellen Falk. My high school English teachers is probably rolling over in her grave at my misplaced modifiers and lack of grammar knowledge. I am a pantser writer and I transcribe the words as the story plays out on stage in my head. Sadly, my characters don't always use the correct words, but Ellen sees that and corrects the poor word choice and order.

Alec

CHAPTER 1

D r. Jill Quint, along with her husband, Nathan Conroy, arrived at the Green Bay, Wisconsin airport in typical late-December weather. She and her friends, Marie, Jo, and Angela were planning Christmas at Jo's house. Jo had a nice house on the bay, and she loved to entertain. Another friend, Henrik Klein, would be arriving aboard his private jet from Germany later that day. They often vacationed together, but this would be their first time visiting the Midwest in winter. Jo also had secured tickets to a Green Bay Packers game for the group of friends.

Winter was unpredictable; some years they had snow in December, and other times, not. This year they were going to be treated to a white Christmas. There had been heavy snowfall a few days before their arrival, but the roads and runways were clear for transportation.

Jo met them at baggage claim, and soon they were in her car and on the way to her home. They turned onto the street leading to the street her house was located on and were blocked by law enforcement vehicles. Fortunately, there was another road she could take to reach her house.

"That's strange. They weren't there when I left for the airport; and besides, that house has been unoccupied for at least two years. I wonder what's going on?"

Jill, a forensic pathologist and licensed private investigator from California, wondered too. She looked at the insignias on the doors of the vehicles, and then she had an inkling.

"They've found a dead body in the house or on the grounds surrounding that house. They've got both police and sheriff, the medical examiner, the power company, and it looks like the water company. They probably have detectives, also."

"Before I moved here, the old gentleman who was the owner died. He was estranged from his family, and the house was ruled uninhabitable. The family does the bare minimum required by the city and pays the taxes. I've wondered why they haven't knocked the house down," Jo said as she pulled into the garage of her house.

They unloaded their suitcases, walked inside to greet a black cat named Beast and a dachshund named Diaper Boy, and dropped their cases in the bedroom they would be staying in. Diaper Boy had never been potty trained by the previous owner and wore a variety of colorful dog diapers.

Nathan asked, "Are you going to resist the call to walk over to that house and find out what's going on?"

"You know me so well, love. I'll see if I can walk Diaper Boy over to the house. Since he's a small dog and low to the ground, I don't know how well he does with winter walks."

They rejoined their hostess in her kitchen and Jill asked, "Can I take Diaper Boy for a walk around the block?"

"Yes, if you put his jacket on. Also, be prepared to carry him at some point as he will sit down and be done with his walk at that time. Are you going to investigate the police activity?"

"Gee whiz, first Nathan and then you are suspecting me of checking out those cars," Jill said with a laugh.

"We know you. Your presence seems to bring on murder. I can't wait to find out what's going on."

Jill nodded. She pulled on winter boots, a hat, gloves, and a warm parka. She slid her PI license into a pocket as well as her physician's license in case the officials wanted to see her identification. With her mid-length blond hair tied back in a ponytail, she and the dog headed out to the abandoned house. She got a little beyond the driveway when Diaper Boy, as predicted, sat down, refusing to walk anymore. She turned around to return to the house, noting that he had peed. She brought him back inside.

She was taking off his jacket and putting on a fresh

diaper when Jo called out from the kitchen, "That was a quick walk."

"As predicted, he sat down a few steps beyond your driveway, so I decided to bring him back inside rather than carry him there and back. He peed and I put a fresh diaper on. I'll walk over on my own."

"See you," Jo said.

Jill walked outside again, watching for icy patches on the road. Fortunately, although there was snow on the ground, the snowplow had recently been through and had dumped salt, so she was walking on dry pavement for the most part. She reached the house in under four minutes, observing from a distance. Some of Jo's neighbors were also standing and watching. Crime scene tape hadn't been strung yet, but there appeared to be a sheriff's deputy on the outside making sure nosy neighbors were kept away. Jill approached the deputy.

"Hello, I'm visiting a friend in this neighborhood for a week. However, I'm a licensed forensic pathologist and PI in another state. Do you need any help or forensic expertise?"

Jill thought the deputy would blow her off, but instead he said, "Stay here and let me ask someone." Then he turned and walked into the house, calling out a name. She guessed she was benefiting from what the region called *Midwest nice.*

Shortly, he came back out with someone trailing him. The man walked around the deputy and assessed her quickly.

Jill pegged him as a detective.

"I understand you're a licensed forensic pathologist from another state. May I see some identification?"

Jill nodded and pulled out her California licenses and passed them over. Then she pulled out FBI Special Agent in Charge Leticia Lopez's business card and added, "If you want to call her office, she will vouch for my expertise."

The man raised his eyebrows at the card and said, "Here's the situation: we have a murder investigation and our county's Medical Examiner is on vacation at the moment. We're waiting for an ME to arrive from Milwaukee, but they won't be here for several hours if at all today. I'm going to verify your credentials, talk with our DA, and then I would appreciate your help."

The detective stepped away to do just that. He had a strange murder scene and really needed the expertise of an ME now. How fortuitous that one was visiting a neighbor. What were the odds of that happening. Five minutes later he had approval from the DA and verification by the FBI of the usefulness of this woman.

He walked over to her and said, "Dr. Quint, I've verified your identity and usefulness. I would appreciate your help. Come with me. I'm Detective Mark Van Lanen."

They walked out of earshot of the neighbors and he began to describe the scene. "We have multiple murder victims at this scene. At least two of them are located in the basement, where a pipe had burst and encased them in ice given the temperature inside the house. We don't know how to remove the remains and not tamper with any potential evidence."

Just then, the detective was called over to a van with a covered boat behind it. The detective motioned Jill to follow him and she did.

They peered inside the van to see another likely victim and then walked back to the boat to find two victims on the floor of the boat with snow on them. The snow must have fallen through holes in the cover.

"Wow, you do need forensic help. Let's go look at the basement and then we can talk about how to remove these remains," Jill said. She took a moment to text Nathan, asking him to bring over the small forensic kit that she traveled with. "I've asked my husband to bring over a mini-forensic kit that I travel with; would you ask the deputy to bring it to me when he arrives?"

"You vacation with a forensic kit?"

"Yes. Murder seems to follow me around the world. In fact, I solved another case with your department about four or five years ago—it was the case of a murdered physician on a golf course. I've had cold-weather murders before, but I've never had a victim encased in ice. Can you tell me about the weather over the past week here?"

"You think these deaths occurred in the last week?"

"The bodies in the van and the boat, based on their state of decomposition despite the cold weather, have been there less than a week. Can the city tell us when the pipes burst here? I assume there would have been a large amount of water dumped into the house and their water usage meters probably noted that."

The detective nodded and wrote that down in his notebook. His phone beeped and then he swiped a few things on it and held it out to Jill.

"Our DA developed a document for you to sign. It is both a confidentiality agreement and a contract to hire you. We'll need those items when the case comes to court."

Jill had expected something like the document and wasn't surprised. She read it over as well as a quoted hourly rate. She was tempted to say that it was not necessary to pay her, but that pay legitimized her presence, and her friends would likely help on the case. Mostly Jill wanted to solve these murders to find justice for these victims and make Jo's neighborhood safer. She was also glad that Diaper Boy had sat down when he had as the dog would have been in the way.

They entered the bone-chillingly cold house that was. It was a very old house, a faded blue on the outside, with choppy rooms on two levels. The wood was rotting around the windows enough that she could see the outside. She followed the detective down a half-flight of steps and then he stopped to turn on a high-powered flashlight.

It was one of the creepiest death scenes she had ever seen. One body was face down and the other was face up. There were dark brown stains on their clothing that likely were blood. The bodies were curled a little. Time of death would be extremely difficult to determine with the weather, the ice, and the position of the bodies. In fact, she couldn't even tell what the murder weapon was, though it was likely a knife or a bullet. She would gain more information during the autopsy, but first they needed to remove these remains. Given the size of the basement, they would need to melt the ice to determine if there were other bodies encased in ice that they couldn't see just yet.

"Do you go ice fishing, Detective Van Lanen?" Jill asked.

The detective looked at her and gave her a look that said, *We're at a murder scene and you're asking me about ice fishing?*

"Yessss," said the detective hesitantly, not knowing where the question was going.

"Could you use whatever tool you use to cut a hole in the ice to cut a box around these victims to remove them from the basement?"

The detective thought about her question for a bit and looked at the clearance between the top of the ice and the ceiling of the basement. There was just enough room for someone to lie on their belly and carve.

"Do you think that is the best way forensically to remove the remains? We could apply heat and melt this basement ice."

"I think that would take a few days to do as I wouldn't want the likely excessive heat needed to melt the ice in this location to affect autopsy findings. It would be better to move the remains to the ME's office and allow them to gradually thaw on an autopsy table."

"Let me talk to a few people and I'll get back to you. Why don't you examine the bodies outside while we figure out what to do here?"

As Jill stepped out of the house she saw Nathan returning to Jo's house and a deputy had her mini-forensic kit. She grabbed it before going over to the van and boat.

She opened the kit, reaching for her gloves. She carried medium and large gloves, though she usually used small gloves to examine remains. She debated taking her winter gloves off versus putting a large pair of latex gloves over the fabric gloves. In the end, she took off the winter gloves and hoped her hands wouldn't freeze before she finished her examination.

CHAPTER 2

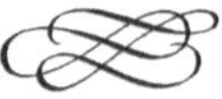

The van had been unlocked, according to the officers nearby. Jill quickly confirmed the victim was dead, though she had not had no doubt about it when she had looked in earlier. Still, she had to officially confirm. Likewise, she did the same for the two victims in the boat. All three victims had body temps in the high 20s so they had been dead for quite a while. Still, she would need to do a number of calculations to determine time of death. The bodies were stiff, but it was long past the time for rigor mortis. Like those encased in ice, these three could likewise thaw out on an autopsy table. These three victims had a variety of stab wounds and Jill guessed that she would find those to be the cause of death. Law enforcement representatives were taking a variety of pictures of the victims before they were removed by the mortuary aides.

Jill felt the vibration of an arriving text; it was Jo asking when she would return. Henrik had arrived and would be at her house in half an hour. Jo planned for dinner to be served in about two hours. Jill looked around the crime scene thinking about the work that needed to be done and the issue of removing the remains. She couldn't do much more at the scene other than to give the mortuary aides instructions for thawing the bodies. As there were at least five victims, and she could begin autopsying them perhaps after three hours. She would check in with the detective as to how he would like to use her services.

She returned to the basement where Detective Van Lanen and some firemen were using saws to work their way through the ice. After they were able to separate the chunk of ice holding each body forever in eternity, the next problem would be how to move the ice block out of the basement. It would be heavy with the weight of the body and the ice surrounding it. They had a narrow doorway to move the block through. As the house was condemned, they could also break out a glass window and move the body out. She would let the firemen figure that out as they likely had the most experience moving humans out of small spaces.

She asked the detective to come away from the noise of the ice saws so she could have a quick conversation. He followed her outside.

"Hi, I've instructed the mortuary aides on what to do with the remains of the victims that are outside. Their body temps were in the 20s so they'll likely need to thaw before we can do an autopsy. As for the ice block victims, they won't be ready for autopsy till tomorrow sometime. I can't think of how I can help you forensically until I do the autopsies. Question for you—is your ME arriving soon from Milwaukee? Do you want me to do some of the autopsies as it will take an ME a while to sort through this number of remains?"

The detective looked around at the scene. Then he checked his email for an update from Milwaukee and did a calculation.

"Dr. Quint, why don't you return to your friends for a couple of hours and then visit the ME's office later tonight to assure us that the thawing process is appropriate. We'll probably be here all night collecting evidence. The Milwaukee ME can't make it here until sometime tomorrow and is content to have you continue in your role and do the autopsies tomorrow. How does that sound?"

Jill took a deep breath. She had no plans with her friends the next day, and five autopsies would be the most she had ever done as a private consultant. However, when she worked for a California county, she had had days when she would do five autopsies, so she knew it was doable.

"I can do as you request. Can you give me a guestimate of when you will be ready to move the basement remains?"

"I honestly have no idea. It's one thing to achieve just cutting the ice block out, it's another to figure out how to move the ice block. It could be fast or slow. Give me your cell number and I'll let you know when we've loaded the remains in the mortuary van."

Jill nodded and they shared contact information. She turned to walk home to her friends and dinner. She was grateful to take off the latex gloves and put on her winter gloves. She arrived at Jo's house about the same time as Henrik, who had rented a car. Henrik was a millionaire computer security CEO who lived in Germany. She went over to give him a hug and they walked into Jo's house together.

Jo came over to give Henrik a hug, adding that Marie and Angela would be there shortly. Then she said to Jill, "So they took you up on your offer of help? When Nathan said he was walking over a kit for you, I knew you'd made inroads with the locals. Obviously, there's a murder victim at the house. Do you know who it is?"

"I signed a contract with the locals to do their ME work. Their normal ME is on vacation and the earliest the Milwaukee ME can drive here is tomorrow sometime. There are at least five victims, all of whom are frozen, so there's not much more I can do this evening. Two of the victims are being cut out of the ice in the basement of the abandoned house."

Jo cut in with, "Five victims in my neighborhood. Oh my gosh!"

"Yeah, this is a new situation for me. I've never had to wait for a victim's remains to thaw before I could perform an autopsy. I also think that's why the local police were so interested in having me on the case, as they had never seen such a condition of a victim's remains and they didn't want to do something that might compromise them forensically."

They entered Jo's house, and Nathan caught the tail-end of Jill's explanation. He walked over to hug Jill and then greeted Henrik before they all gathered at Jo's kitchen island. It was a large sparkly slab of marble.

"Are you sure they were murdered? Maybe it was a gas leak or something," Nathan suggested.

"No, there are visible stab wounds on the victims in the van and boat. The ones encased in ice in the basement have something brown on their clothing."

"Encased in ice in a basement? How will you get them out? I'm imagining a large pond with dead humans inside," Henrik said with a wince.

"Try an ice fishing saw," Jo suggested.

Angela walked inside Jo's kitchen, asking what the saw was for. After everyone had time for a greeting and hug, they repeated their question looking outside at the snow. The bay hadn't frozen yet, so there was no ice fishing.

Jill took over the conversation. "Were there a bunch of emergency lights when you arrived in Jo's neighborhood?"

Angela nodded.

"There were murder victims discovered in that house."

Angela interrupted, "Victims? As in more than one?"

Jill nodded, "There are at least five, and two are

encased in ice in the basement. Law enforcement is using ice fishing saws to cut the victims out of the ice so they can be moved to the Medical Examiner's office. As the county ME is away from the area on vacation, they've hired me until they can get the Milwaukee ME here. So we'll all have something to do over the holiday."

"That's really sad. Prayers for those victims," Angela said. "Why did you say 'at least five'?"

"The pipes burst in the house and the basement is frozen, so once we remove the two bodies we can see, and melt the ice, there may be more. Hopefully not," Jill said crossing her fingers. "There are an additional two bodies in a boat and one in the van the boat is attached to. They'll be moved to the ME's office and I will head there this evening after dinner to see if the three bodies found outside are thawed enough for an autopsy. Even after they cut the ice the around the other two victims in the basement, it will be difficult to remove them from the house, so I won't get to those two until tomorrow."

"This sounds like one of the most gruesome cases we've had so far," Angela said. "Jill, how did you get involved so quickly, and Jo, what's wrong with your neighborhood?"

All eyes turned to Jo, who shrugged and said, "This is a very diverse neighborhood. We have million-dollar homes and we have $200,000 homes. One of our streets has a meth dealer who has been in and out of jail. He would be my first suspect."

"How do you know you have a meth dealer here, and where is he located?" Henrik asked.

"His house is on Sprout Lane, which is about a block and a half from here. It's the talk of the neighborhood, confirmed by public reporting and the fact that the SWAT team arrested him. It was kind of hard to miss. One of his neighbors asked us to come with her to the Town Board and request that the house be bulldozed because it was a health hazard. I said no, it doesn't work that way. I think he distributes meth, but he doesn't cook the meth there, so the town can't do that even if they were interested in doing so."

"I normally do a tox screen as part of any autopsy and test for meth among other illegal substances. I'll also look for the signs of meth use like tooth and skin decay. I wonder if he's one of the victims, if he is not the murderer. They're all unidentifiable until they thaw."

"That sounds like someone pulling meat out to thaw after being in the freezer. What a terrible crime scene," Angela said. "I'm glad that when we assist you, we don't see crime scene pictures or dead bodies."

Jill rubbed Angela's shoulder and said, "Your talents lie elsewhere in terms of crime solving. You don't need to see the murder victim in order to help us solve the case. You contribute in other ways."

"Your occupation seems particularly filled with grossness with this case," Jo said.

"Yes, there are more victims than I usually deal with on our cases, but it is a Midwest winter that makes the case seem worse when we think about being encased in ice. From my point of view, the ice performs a service for me of preserving evidence, although if the police wanted to do a fingerprint scan to identify the victims, the ridges on their fingers have changed thanks to the condition of the bodies. As a pathologist, I'll take the effects of ice over heat. Is that too much information?" Jill asked of her friends.

"Let's not eat dinner anytime soon," Angela replied.

"Let's change the topic and catch up on everyone's lives," Jill said as Marie walked in.

"What topic are you changing from?" she asked as everyone groaned.

"If you drove by the police activity on the way here, then you know that I and maybe we—have a new case," Jill said as Marie walked over to Henrik to hug and kiss him. They were in a long-distance relationship that was moving extremely slow in the eyes of her friends.

"Okay, what's new in everyone's lives?" Jo asked. "I should mention some plans I've made while you all are here. We'll be taking in a Green Bay Packers game, touring the Festival of Lights at the Botanical Garden, taking in a Christmas concert at St. Norbert Abbey, playing pickleball, and volunteering at the food bank on Christmas Day. Everyone can opt in or out for each activity."

"Phew," Angela said. "You know I don't have the hand-eye coordination to play pickleball, so I'll opt out of that activity."

"Wow, you've got the week planned. Those are great activities, Jo. Thanks for making all the arrangements."

"Little did I know that murder would get in the way," she muttered, but then smiled.

"It seems to happen whenever you gather as a group," Henrik said.

"Yeah, it's Jill's fault. Murder is attracted to her like a magnet to a refrigerator," Marie said.

"I would deny that, but we've worked on about twenty cases together, so that would be futile on my part," Jill said. "Also, let me say this if I haven't said it enough before: I appreciate all that you've done over the years to help me solve cases and bring justice to the victims."

"Yeah, yeah, and thank you for paying us for many of these cases; we have a nice vacation account now," Marie said, giving Jill a hug.

"Thanks, Marie. I enjoy solving these cases, but I know it's not your first choice of what to do with your spare time, so thanks for helping me."

"We certainly meet interesting people, and I, at least have learned something about financial systems the world over. We also met this geeky character, Henrik, whose computer systems should scare everyone," Jo said, smiling at Henrik.

The group of friends moved on to talk about news in their lives and the plans for the next few days. Then Jill's cellphone rang with a Green Bay area code. She answered it with a cautious, "This is Dr. Quint," and was relieved to hear the detective's voice.

"Dr. Quint, we've managed to remove all of the remains outdoors as well as the first victim encased in ice. The victims are on their way to the ME's office. So if you would like to drive over there soon, you can review that the process for thawing the bodies gives us the best forensic evidence and is respectful to the remains. I would appreciate your supervision."

"Thank you, Detective. I'll leave now." She wrote down the address that the detective gave her.

She turned to the group after she ended the call and said, "I'm going to head over to the ME's office and check the conditions of the thawing bodies, and then I'll be back. I can't imagine I'll be more than an hour so this shouldn't delay our dinner plans. Jo, do you need me to pick up anything on the way home?"

"No. I stocked up this morning, so we're good here. If you do get delayed, text me."

"Will do," Jill said, wrapping herself up in winter clothing to make the drive. She set the address of the office into her phone, went out to Jo's car, and left to attend to the remains.

She arrived at a boring concrete building that housed the Medical Examiner's office and walked inside, quickly unzipping her parka. She had her identification ready so she could be let inside the department. It was a small suite with four autopsy tables. As she wasn't doing the autopsy yet, she stayed in her street clothes. The victims recovered from the van and the boat occupied three of the tables, and the block of ice encasing the fourth victim had been placed on the floor near a drain.

She thought about the position of the victim on the floor and contamination of forensic evidence. She didn't like to think about what other fluids had washed into that drain. She looked around for another solution. The autopsy suite fortunately had a large, wide stretcher for those deceased who were morbidly obese at the time of their death. She decided to have the staff position the victim encased in ice on it after it was cleaned. This would greatly reduce contamination caused by the drain. She assisted the staff in positioning the block of ice onto the stretcher and strapped it into place.

This left the unused autopsy table available for what hopefully is the last victim when they arrived. She would ask the staff to check on the remains throughout the night to make sure they stayed put in their respective spaces as they thawed. Surely in this part of the country, these were not the first sets of remains this morgue had experienced that were frozen. People fell through ice or died outdoors after heavy drinking. However, given the dried blood on the victims' clothing, these were surely homicides rather than accidental winter deaths, and more care would need to be given to forensic evidence. She took the temperatures of the remains of the people who had been outdoors, and they were still below freezing. She asked the staff to take the temperatures hourly, calculating that in another two hours or so the outdoor remains would be above the freezing point and blood could be withdrawn from their veins at that point. Given the number of victims for her to autopsy, she would be back early in the morning to check their condition and proceed with the autopsies.

She took a final look at the remains, running down a list in her head of what else she could do to protect forensic evidence and be respectful toward the remains. She had left written instructions for the morgue attendants and couldn't think of anything else to do. She bundled back up in her winter outerwear and returned to Jo's car for the drive back to her house. She might need a rental car rather than relying on borrowing someone's car each time she went out, she mused. Tomorrow she would likely lose most of the day to autopsies even if the detective found no more remains in the basement.

CHAPTER 3

*J*ill arrived back at Jo's house just as the group was putting the finishing touches on the preparation of their meal. Henrik had brought wines from the vineyard he owned in Germany. Marie and Angela brought salad and dessert. Nathan and Jo's partner, Matthew, cooked the meat dishes. Everyone contributed to the meal except Jill, which was fine with her. Unlike her husband and group of friends, she hated cooking.

They sat down, toasting their friendship, the meal, and the holiday season. They caught up on each other's lives. Finally, they circled back to the mystery at hand—the murders in Jo's neighborhood.

Henrik asked, "Are these the most unusual murder victims you've had to care for?"

Jill thought back to her career in a California County Medical Examiner's office as well as her private cases and said, "Sadly, no. I think the case in Australia and New Zealand a few years ago takes the cake for the weirdest. I don't know if we ever told you about that case?"

"I remember that you, Nathan, and I think Angela vacationed there and there was a string of deaths that followed, but I don't remember more than that."

"In a nutshell, a forensic expert from Australia went off the rails when he was cancelled as a speaker at a forensic conference and was replaced by me. I had no idea that I had replaced someone. He set about trying to prove that I was no expert by laying a trail of murder victims and attempted murders to see if I would notice them and could solve them. He used many of the deadly animals of those two countries for murder, as well as poison and a zip line sabotage. It took law enforcement from both countries to solve the case. He'll spend the rest of his life in prison in Australia. Of course, you were there for the ice arrow murder in Toronto, Henrik, although if I recall, you and Nathan were drinking beer and didn't witness the actual murder."

"I had forgotten about those cases. I guess you've handled multiple victim murder cases in the past and the only thing that makes this unusual is the cold and ice," Marie said.

"Yeah, that about sums it up, and the fact that it's in Jo's neighborhood. I'll probably be occupied most of tomorrow doing the autopsies, so I'm glad the Packers game is scheduled for the next day."

"Do you need to borrow one of our cars?" Jo asked.

"I was thinking of getting a rental car so I don't take a car away from you guys. If someone could run me to the car rental at the airport tonight, I'll just pick one up. It's no big deal and better than inconveniencing anyone here."

"I'll take you later on my way home," Angela said.

"Awesome. Thank you."

The evening was drawing down and the friends represented about nine hours' time zone difference between Jill and Nathan's California and Henrik's Germany. Still with more wine, they continued the conversation while playing a card game. Then Henrik and Marie left to return to her house, followed by Angela taking Jill to get her rental car.

Nathan, Jo, and Matthew were all night owls and were still up talking when Jill returned with the car. She kissed Nathan on the cheek and went to bed knowing she would be awake hours before the three of them.

She crept out of the house the next morning, trying not to make any noise, but Diaper Boy heard her and barked. She quieted him and Beast the cat with dried fish treats and left the house. She was grateful that it hadn't snowed overnight, so the windshield and roads were clear. She arrived at the Medical Examiner's office a short time later. She was buzzed in and shown to a locker room where she could change into scrubs. She then returned to the morgue to assess what was going on with her victims.

The outdoor victims from the van and boat had completely thawed with body temperatures mirroring the room temperature. Both victims who had been encased in ice were still thawing, though the one that had arrived the previous night might be warm enough by the time she completed her autopsies on the first three. During the night, body temperatures were recorded, and blood work was taken and was being processed by a contracted laboratory.

Jill spent the next few hours documenting the cause of death of the outdoor victims. Essentially, all three had sustained mortal wounds somewhere else and were dumped after death into the van or boat. Surprisingly, the blood work came back negative for any drugs.

Given Jo's explanation of the neighborhood meth dealer, Jill would have put her money on these victims being related to that activity. The detective arrived as she was closing up the third victim. He looked tired, as he likely had been at the cold and dark scene most of the night.

"Hello, Detective. I should have asked you if you wanted me to start these autopsies without you. I just assumed you were up most of the night at the crime scene."

"I was there most of the night. Besides the difficulty of removing the bodies from the basement, we needed to try to determine if there were other remains. We don't think so, but as you can imagine from that scene, it was dark and frozen, and I'll be returning to the house after I'm finished here."

"Good luck with that. I have the results of the first three victims. They all sustained mortal wounds from a serrated knife. They were moved to the van or boat sometime before rigor mortis. Their tox screens came back negative for illicit drugs, but I don't have all the lab results yet. I was surprised about the lack of illicit drugs as I understand from my friend who lives in the neighborhood that a meth dealer lives on one of its streets."

"Yes. He is well known to us and was at the top of our suspect list, but we determined that he was in jail over the past three days, so we know it was not him. Were you able to ascertain the time of death?"

"I've performed some calculations of temperature and body chemical tests, and I estimate the deaths of the first three victims occurred about five days ago for the outside victims. That may also be true for the two victims inside the house—they were dumped on the basement floor, but gases inside their remains caused them to rise as water filled the basement from the broken pipe."

"So, my meth dealer might still be a suspect."

"Yes, if he wasn't in jail at the time. Otherwise that's a pretty solid alibi. However, considering that none of these victims so far had any illicit drugs in their system that would sharply reduce the connection to the meth dealer. Are there any other felons in that neighborhood?"

"We haven't done that search yet. I see that the morgue attendants sent fingerprint cards over to the department. We don't have identification for them yet, but hopefully we will by the end of the day."

"Actually, I might be able to help there. I'm with a group of friends to celebrate Christmas. One of our friends is Henrik Klein, who runs a worldwide security software firm that many law enforcement agencies have purchased software from. I'll take pictures of the victims and send them to him, and he'll have them identified in under ten minutes, if you would like. I can guarantee his confidentiality."

"You're surprisingly easy to work with, Dr. Quint. I took a risk yesterday bringing you on, but you come with a lot of unexpected resources. I'll need your friend to sign an agreement for when the case goes to court and to cover our bases. Does he need to be paid for his time?"

"No, he'll do it for free. I actually have a copy of his software on my laptop and could do the same work for you, but he's got a mega-computer in the sky and will be faster. In fact, let me see if he's available right now."

She texted Henrik and found he could run the search for them. She took pictures with her cell phone and sent them to him while the detective waited. Within five minutes, they had the first three victims identified.

"Wow. This has never happened so fast for me. I'll ask my department to contact him to understand what he provides."

"Green Bay isn't a huge town, and I would think you quickly identify most of your victims. As I recall, you have only one or two murders each year, so you may not need the services his software provides, but I consult all over the world, so his software has helped me identify all of my victims so far."

"That's quite a ringing endorsement, but I'm not the decision maker of my department. Besides identification, does he have criminal information on people?"

"Generally, yes. Would you like me to ask him for that?"

"Yes. This will speed up my job. I'll find it out eventually, but I can work faster if I'm just verifying what's he's given me rather than independently searching all of our databases."

Jill nodded and sent another text to Henrik. She added that he might be getting a call regarding his system from the department. He responded with his usual offer of a job as Chief Marketer for his software. She smiled and then asked the morgue attendant if there was a printer nearby. She was able to connect her phone to the printer via Bluetooth and printed the information on each of the victims that Henrik sent.

The information was surprisingly slim. None of the victims had criminal records. They were Wisconsin residents, but not all were from Green Bay or its suburbs. The detective thanked her for the information and asked her when she might identify the two victims encased in ice.

Jill walked over to the body that was still thawing to study the facial features. There were no good camera angles and she suspected the body had been dumped on the basement floor and left in the position it had fallen in, which was curled on its side. While the ice had melted around some of the face, it wasn't completely uncovered yet. She grabbed a blow dryer which every autopsy suite contained and turned it on to finish melting the ice around the face. There was no forensic evidence to be found on the face. With the ice gone from around the cheeks, the question was, how much did the cheeks change once the tissues underneath the skin thawed as well? She took pictures and sent them to Henrik knowing that the victim might be misidentified or unidentified because she had the wrong cheek structure, but she would give it a try.

"I've sent the pictures off to my friend, but while I melted the ice around the face, the tissues underneath remain frozen and may change shape once they're thawed. So if he can't identify the victim or he comes back with an identity, take it with a grain of salt."

Her phone pinged, and she pulled up the text. The software identified a few matches with a low level of accuracy. Henrik recommended waiting until she could get better images of the deceased.

"My friend's software has made matches, but they come with a low level of accuracy. I can share this with you or you can wait perhaps another hour or two for me to get a thawed image of this victim."

"I'll wait. I've got enough to research without chasing down potentially bad information. I'll need to do family notifications, and that will likely take me to the time that new information becomes available for the fourth victim."

"Okay, Detective, I'll send you identification notification as soon as I get it. The last victim's identity won't be ready until this evening, though."

The detective left and Jill returned to her two ice-encrusted victims. She wondered about using a blade saw used to cut the skull open—could she use it to shave away some of the ice from the face of the fifth victim to accelerate the melting and thus identification? She took the saw and tried it on the ice. It worked, so she asked the morgue attendant to grab a second saw and assist with cutting away more of the ice. She wished she'd thought of that earlier. Half an hour later, she felt satisfied that she had greatly reduced the thawing time of the final two victims.

The fourth victim had thawed sufficiently around the head that she took new pictures and sent them to Henrik. This time they came with a single match and high rate of accuracy. He included additional information, and again this victim didn't have a criminal history. He was also a Wisconsin resident, but from a city about a half-hour away called Pulaski. She forwarded the information to the detective and then returned to the man to take his core temperature. He was still too cold to draw blood. She looked around and determined that she had at least two hours before the victims' core temperatures rose sufficiently to begin work on them. She decided to go home and return once they were more thoroughly thawed.

CHAPTER 4

*J*ill arrived in time for lunch, which was mostly leftovers from the previous evening. That suited her as it was a delicious meal, and she didn't have a lot of time before she returned to the ME's office.

All of her friends were gathering for dinner that evening at a local restaurant, and she would meet them there after she finished the final two autopsies. She gave the names of the first three victims to her friends to see what they could find and how they were connected. Jo was relieved that none of the victims were her neighbors. She didn't know everyone who lived in her neighborhood, so she wouldn't necessarily have known that someone was missing. She went to work looking for financial records before they dined that evening. Jill knew the detective would also be doing that, but her team often found more information than the detectives. Marie was also doing her usual dossier on each of the victims. Jill was grateful that Marie, Jo, and Angela had the week off work to accommodate their social activities, or in this case to help her solve these murders. Tomorrow they would be tailgating before the football game, so much of the day was lost. At least she would finish the autopsies by this evening, and maybe the Milwaukee Medical Examiner would be available to co-sign her work as a pathologist licensed in the state of Wisconsin.

Jill headed back to Medical Examiner's office to begin the autopsy on the fourth victim. It was like doing an autopsy on a victim that was fetched from the water, as there was no other way to describe it other than soggy. The bodies would have floated in the water perhaps two or three days before it turned to ice based on the water company reports and the temperatures. Still, she was prepared to examine the remains found in this water-logged condition. Again, she confirmed death by stabbing with a serrated knife. And again, blood work came back with no illicit drugs.

All of the victims were between forty and fifty years of age. The stab wounds appeared to be to the chest as though the murderer had kept stabbing the victim until they struck the heart, resulting in death. She was unable to determine if these frozen victims were killed inside the basement or moved there, as she couldn't see the size of the pool of blood from the stab wounds, but based on her estimated time of death and the position of the body, she assumed that they were dumped there after they had been dead for at least an hour.

She moved onto the final victim just as the Medical Examiner arrived from Milwaukee. He quickly went over the reports she had already completed, pulling out the remains from each cooler. He co-signed the report findings and then joined her for the final case. He was in a hurry to leave as reduced staffing for the holidays meant that he was the only ME available for the large city of Milwaukee. Unfortunately, human beings hadn't stopped killing each other, and he had cases and detectives waiting for him 100 miles to the south. He co-signed the last report.

"I'm so grateful you happen to be here on vacation and have the right credentials and experience to competently handle these autopsies. Why does everyone in the state have to die around the holidays when we are supposed to be full of good cheer and happiness?"

"I remember back in my old job when some holidays resulted in a low murder rate and other years seem to be full of people with murderous intentions. You're just having bad luck this year."

"With a little good luck that you were in the area and on hand to help. How did you come to be involved?"

"I'm visiting a friend who lives around the corner from the murder location and on the ride home from the airport, I could see the police activity. I walked over and volunteered to help. I think if the state wasn't so short staffed, and the murders so unusual, they might have waited until more resources became available, but who can argue with a random forensic pathologist who happens to be on the scene?"

"Well, thank you again for your service, but I've got to run. Great work, Dr. Quint."

Jill nodded as he turned to rush out the door, calling out, "Safe travels!" He waved just before he left.

She finished sewing up the last victim and saw him returned to the cooler. Henrik was able to identify the fifth victim and his particulars, which she forwarded to the detective along with the final autopsy paperwork. With her work done, she returned to the locker room to shower, change, looking at her watch. It was perfect timing to meet up with her friends at the restaurant.

She arrived at the parking lot at the same time as Marie and Henrik, and they walked in together; Angela arrived shortly afterward. They had come to expect Jo to be late to any social occasion and she didn't disappoint this time; she was the last to arrive, along with the other two men.

"Henrik, thanks for your work identifying the victims," Jill said. "I told the detective I had the same software on my laptop, but you had a super-duper sky computer that was faster. He was forwarding your name to his higher-ups, so hopefully you or one of your team members will return here to sell them on the system."

"You could accept employment with my company

and fly in to see your friends and do the presentation for me."

"Yeah, but then I would have to learn all the bells and whistles of what your software does for law enforcement rather than my corner of it. I think I do a better job connecting officers to your company and then getting out of the middle. How's that working for you?" Jill said with a smile.

"Really well, actually. I think we've secured contracts with 100% of the agencies referred by you. I guess what I need you to do is to get involved with more murder cases. Then I could double my contracts," Henrik suggested.

"No thanks. I wouldn't have time to enjoy the company of my friends and make wine." Jill operated a vineyard in California focused on the muscat grape, though she recently had expanded into five new wines.

"That is true. Too bad."

They noticed Jo, Matthew, and Nathan arrive and waved them over. Nathan leaned into kiss her before settling down in a seat next to her.

"How was your day?" he asked.

"Sad, but I'm finished. Now it's up to the detectives to make notifications to the victims' families and solve the case."

"Really? You and your friends are not doing your own research?"

"Well, of course we are. Unless a bus crashed and somehow dumped the five victims into the boat, the van, and the basement, you know I don't like unsolved mysteries. There were five people stabbed to death from different suburbs near Green Bay, and I need to know why. Besides, I thought this would be an open-and-shut case with Jo's local meth dealer, but all five victims had no trace of any illicit drugs or arrest records. So now it's up to us to find justice for these victims."

"Nathan, did you really expect some other answer?" Jo asked.

"Nope, I was just clarifying what we'll be doing in our spare time here on vacation."

"We just need to find a location to travel where Jill can't find dead bodies."

"A deserted island?" Marie suggested.

"Look at this way: we're just making the neighborhood safe for Jo and Matthew again. As our besties, we wouldn't want them to be in danger when they walk their dog or cat."

"Wait, Jo, did I hear correctly?, Do you walk your cat?" Henrik asked, puzzled.

Jo grinned and said, "Of course I take Beast for walks. I bought a baby stroller with a zip-up netting around it and he enjoys our walks."

"You Americans are crazy."

"Crazy about our animals; yes we are," Jo said.

The waiter came to take their drink order, and they deferred to Nathan to order for the group. He was the one with the deepest knowledge of wines as he insisted on tasting any wine before he designed its label for the winery. He had recently expanded into beer labels and was gaining expertise in beer varietals. He knew what everyone planned to order for dinner and matched the wine to the menu choice.

After the wine was brought, tasted and poured, they ordered their meal. Once everyone was out of earshot they pressed Jill for more information about the strange case in Jo's neighborhood.

"We have five people stabbed to death in the chest with the killing wound to the heart. They were killed elsewhere and moved to the house, probably about an hour or two after their death and before rigor mortis. They don't seem to be related, and they are all negative for illicit drugs. That's all I know at the moment. Jo was going to investigate the financials and Marie was evaluating their social media posts."

"I haven't found anything unusual in the financials. They all have paid their property taxes where they own land. No one has as much as a speeding ticket. They work at a variety of jobs. They just seem like a random group of people," Jo said with a shrug, and turned to look at Marie, as though she would have the answers in her social media evaluation.

"I didn't see anything in their posts either. They weren't friends, and while one or two had a friend in common, there was not a single person among them who was friends with all of them. It's as though they were randomly picked for murder."

They were interrupted by the wait staff as they brought special utensils needed for their different dinner orders. Nathan took a moment to talk about the wine varietals they were drinking until the staff disappeared.

"Good change in conversation, Babe. Thank you. We don't want the staff hearing our conversation. Hopefully, you can keep that up all night," Jill said.

He smiled at his wife, knowing his duty in investigations.

"Have the police announced the murders yet?" Angela asked.

"I don't know if they have made all the family notifications yet as we didn't identify the last victim until about three hours ago. Does anyone have a local news app that they can open to see?" Jill said.

There was silence as Jo, Marie, and Angela did quick searches to learn that the murders were being announced.

"Yeah, the police have announced that they found remains; no names have been released pending family notifications, and they have no suspects yet, but there is a person of interest. I'm guessing that's my neighborhood meth dealer. I think you said he was in jail recently, but it wasn't an alibi for the time of the murders," Jo said.

"No, he doesn't have an alibi for their time of death. I also think the suspect has to be very strong or had help to move dead bodies from where they were killed to the boat, van, and basement. Have you seen your meth neighbor? Is he strong enough to move bodies?"

"I haven't seen him, but I hear he's in his early 50s and slight, so I doubt he could carry the victims any distance. He must not do meth himself as he would be dead by now. Still, how much did each of these victims weigh?"

They were interrupted by food service and the conversation switched to Henrik talking about his progress with the vineyard he had purchased a few years ago. In silent agreement, they stayed on the subject of wine until everyone had finished their soup or salad. Plates were removed and the main courses were delivered.

The conversation stayed on wine and beer until they were well through their main courses. No one had room for dessert, but they did enjoy a second glass of wine as they sat chatting.

"Okay, friends, we need to solve these murders in the next three days before Jill leaves. We've done well solving cases all over the world, and this is in my own backyard so to speak. I and my neighbors deserve to have our neighborhood made safe."

"Wow, talk about pressure," Henrik said. "I don't envy you, Jill, but then again, I've watched you over the years create investigative miracles while solving cases."

"I haven't done that alone; it's been us as a group. We usually attract the attention of the killer, and that always helps us solve the case though it puts us in danger. Let's examine the location where these murdered victims were found and talk about that, or maybe we can adjourn to Marie's house as it is the closest so we don't have to worry about anyone over-hearing our conversation."

The group agreed with that idea and wrapped up dinner, paid their bill, and soon departed. A short time later, they were situated in Marie's living room with water for the drivers and wine for the passengers.

"So, that house has been deserted for two years, you say?" Jill asked.

"Yes. Bones, as he was known in the neighborhood, grew old, in that house. We would see him with his walker and his closest neighbors brought him food. Then one day he wasn't there anymore, and I heard he had passed. The house has just sat there empty and decaying since. In the summer, the town has forced the family to do minimal landscaping, but otherwise there's been no activity. As the house faces the forty-seven-acre green-space owned by the university, there's no one to observe comings and goings unless you happen to drive by the house at the right time. The streets are not well lit here, so in the middle of the night it would be easy to deliver a body without anybody seeing you. Of course, you would need to know that the house was abandoned. It looks abandoned from the outside, and I believe there's a notice on one of the doors that says the house is not habitable, but I've never tried to walk through the weeds to actually find out what the notice says. The windows are not boarded up, but the derelict condition would hint that no one lives there or that it's just a summer cottage."

"Have you tried the doors on the house? Are they locked?" Jill asked.

"No. I don't go around trying the doors on abandoned houses. I've seen that go wrong in too many horror movies. Mostly, I think that it's none of my business," Jo said.

"So, there are some houses in your neighborhood that face the five roads. I wonder if they have any front-door cameras that record activity on that street," Nathan suggested.

"I'll ask them tomorrow. I would have thought the police would ask them as well," Jo said.

"I would think the police have been involved in processing forensic information and investigating the suspects. I would guess they'll be canvassing the neighborhood tomorrow for information. I haven't heard from the detective if the basement has been completely thawed yet to verify that we have all the victims," Jill said.

Everyone frowned at the thought that there could be more victims.

"There are so many places to dump bodies around this state. If the person had trampled through the snow and dumped the bodies in the greenspace, the bodies likely wouldn't be discovered for a much longer time," Marie said.

"I bet the person thought they were safe dumping them where they did as there's been no activity in that house for a long time. Also, you wouldn't leave a path through the snow dripping blood as you walked. The branches are thick, and I would think that it would not be an easy walk," Henrik said.

"That's a little too graphic, Henrik," Angela said wrinkling her nose.

"Yes, but you get my point. These bodies potentially would have sat there for another two years rotting away except for the pipes bursting, so that was a bad piece of luck."

"To me, leaving the bodies on that property suggests a familiarity with the neighborhood. So either someone who lives there, visits there, or makes frequent deliveries and sees the lack of activity at that house or knows its story," Jill said.

Silence greeted Jill as everyone thought through her statement.

Jo spoke first. "Much as I would like to disagree with your statement, I think you're right, Jill. I'm good friends with the couple on the corner as you come into this development and I know the people in the house next to them. They may be gone at the moment as they spend some time each winter snowbirding in a warmer climate."

Snowbirds were North Americans who went to warmer climates to escape the harsh Midwestern and Canadian winters.

"So if they aren't away, we'll talk with them first thing in the morning," Jill said, looking at Angela since she was their best interviewer.

"I can do one better as I have their email address. I'll send them an email right now asking if they have a doorbell camera and a subscription that shows the activity from a week ago. What's your best guess on when the bodies were dumped at the house?" Jo said, then added. "*Dump* is a harsh word. Perhaps I should say *placed*."

Jill shrugged as she could think of far harsher words like *abandoned, discarded,* or *disposed of.* "That would be great. I'm guessing that the bodies have been there less than a week, so we would want to start with footage from the middle of the night for four to seven days ago."

There was silence as Jo typed out an email on her phone and then she looked up after she hit the Send button.

"Jo, how about the other houses on that street or the side street?"

"I don't know the other couple on the corner, so we would have to knock on the door and introduce ourselves. As for the side street, they don't face the driveway, so even if they had door cameras, it wouldn't be the right angle. The guy at the end of my street can view that house, but his front door faces away from the house. We'll scout the neighborhood in the morning. What do you think the detectives will be doing?"

"It depends on how many are assigned to this case. As it is the holidays, there are likely a reduced number of them, and I think they would be interviewing family members to determine when their loved ones went missing. If the basement has been completely defrosted and pumped out, then they likely have already collected any forensic evidence from the scene and they won't return to this neighborhood until tomorrow."

"Remember, we have the game tomorrow and it's a three-ish kick-off, so we'll need to leave for the stadium around noon," Angela said, and everyone nodded.

Jill stood up and said, "I'm ready to head home. It's been a long day and those are the most remains I've autopsied in one day in a long time. I'm ready to drop."

The group broke up and shortly everyone went their separate ways, with Jo and Matthew leading Jill and Nathan back to her house. Jill had Nathan slow down as they drove by the deserted house in the dark. She could barely make out the crime scene tape strung around the van, boat, and house doors. The entire scene looked so sad.

They walked into the house, and Jill said her good-nights as Nathan elected to stay and chat with Jo and Matthew a little longer. He was a night owl, so it was not unexpected. Jill fell asleep thinking about the details of the case and what she could investigate next.

CHAPTER 5

Jill was up early and took a walk around Jo's neighborhood looking for exterior cameras. It was around 20 degrees Fahrenheit. The sun was out, and it was expected to warm up to the high 30s by game time. Unlike Jill's California sun, the winter sun in Wisconsin made the temperatures cooler, as there was no cloud cover to hold the heat in. Still sunshine made her happy. It would be a glorious day for football.

She took her cellphone out and zoomed in on the houses that fronted the street in the neighborhood looking for exterior cameras. Many of the houses didn't have them. In fact, Jo's house had a camera, but it didn't save footage as she didn't have a subscription anymore, so even if there was a camera in the right place, it didn't mean that it would have saved the footage.

At the end of her walk, she concluded that the only

camera that might be of use was the one on the corner that Jo had emailed the previous night and the couple next to them who might not be home. She returned to Jo's house in hopes that Jo was awake. Matthew was in the kitchen making coffee for her, so she would get an answer soon.

Jill walked into Jo's bedroom to find her sitting up with bedhead hair and an iPad on her lap. She took a seat on a chair.

"Good morning! Did you get a response to your email?" Jill asked.

"Gee whiz, give a girl a moment with her coffee before you start firing questions at her."

"Gee whiz back at you. Would you expect anything else from me?"

Matthew walked in and passed the coffee to Jo before retreating.

"Is Nathan awake yet?"

"You know he won't be up for another hour or so," Jill said, looking at her watch. "How late did you guys stay up talking?"

"We called it quits at midnight, and I got an email back from my neighbors before then. They were going to get some help figuring out their footage. They do have a subscription, so it is saved somewhere, but they've never accessed old footage before and need to learn the process."

"That's good news. Is that something you can help them with since you used to have a subscription?"

"Maybe. I bet Marie or Henrik would be faster to

help them. Marie because she has the same system, and Henrik because he's all things computer."

"That's an excellent suggestion. Let me contact them and see if I can get them over here to help the couple. What are the couple's names?"

"They're Mark and Mary. They're super nice and have a summer party on their back or front lawn every summer with live music. They're walkers, so you might see them out later as the pavement is dry. If it's at all icy, then they stay home and stay safe."

"Got it. Can you send them an email and tell them that Marie, Henrik, and I will stop by around 10 to help them with the footage?"

"Yes. I might even make it out of bed to go with you."

"I'll warn you that it's pretty cold out there," Jill said.

"I love the cold. I'm not worried about it on the short walk there. Tell Marie and Henrik to get here by quarter of 10 and we'll walk over as a group. I have some cookies to deliver to them, so I'll kill two birds with one stone so to speak, though I guess I shouldn't use the term *kill anything* during a murder investigation."

Jill nodded and stood up. "I'll let you continue to wake up and get dressed. I'll be out in the kitchen eating breakfast and checking my emails. Maybe the detective will give me some information if I ask the right way."

"Good luck with that," Jo said as Jill exited the bedroom.

Out in the kitchen, she looked for Matthew, but he must have gone downstairs where his work computer was located. He taught accounting at a local technical college, and even though the school was on a holiday break, there was still work to be done with grades and curriculum for the upcoming semester.

Jill called Marie and relayed the new information about Jo's neighborhood and their 10 am appointment with the couple. Marie confirmed that they would be at Jo's house at the appointed time. That completed, Jill worked on breakfast for herself and then wrote and rewrote an email to the detective in an effort to get new information out of him.

Detective Van Lanen, I normally bring several services to a murder case when private citizens or public agencies hire me. This is what I learned yesterday and this morning and I wondered if you would share any information with me about the victims as you've interviewed their families.

Jill also added in a reference to another law enforcement officer from her last Green Bay murder investigation, so the detective wouldn't think she was a loose cannon. Most law enforcement officers did their best to block her access to information about an investigation, and she suspected this case would be no different, but she could always try to worm information out of him.

Her email was still unanswered by the time that Jo was up and dressed and Marie and Henrik had arrived. Nathan was just beginning to rouse, but he would stay home while their small group approached the neighbors. They left him to find his wakeful state and walked to Mark and Mary's house.

They knocked on the door and were greeted by a smiling Mary. Mark was seated at their kitchen table with a laptop. He looked slightly worried though as he didn't have the footage ready to roll for them. Jo performed introductions and then Mark moved out of the way for Henrik to work his magic with accessing security footage.

A short time later they had the sought after footage for the timeline they desired. In all the nights, only one car arrived after midnight each night, and that was the daughter of one of the neighbors who worked in a bar. So she was ruled out.

"Darn," Jill said. "I was so hopeful that it would be on camera."

"You know it's not the only way to drive to Bones' house," Mark said. "Your person of interest could have come down Grove Street and turned onto one of the other two streets to reach the house."

Jo nodded and replied, "That's true, Mark. Great suggestion. It's funny how focused we were on a single way to reach the house without giving any considera-tion to alternate paths. Especially if the suspect came from the north, going by your house would not have been the best route. We'll walk back by the houses on Grove to see if we can determine who might have a doorbell camera."

"The other thing you could look at is a bird or

squirrel camera. I know that Mike and Kristy have one on their tree, and it likely has a wide angle of the street."

"Good suggestion, Mark. Thanks," Jill said.

The group left and Jo directed them toward Mike and Kristy's house. The garage door was open as Mike was always in his workshop making something out of wood. Jo led the group and said hi to Mike once he looked up from his work. You never wanted to interrupt a man holding a saw for fear he might cut himself.

Jo made quick introductions, and they commiserated over the deaths of someone in their neighborhood. Kristy joined them and pulled out her phone to look at the bird camera and determine if it caught activity on the street. It did capture cars, but not in a readable manner. Still, it was better than nothing. Henrik went to work and soon had the night footage pulled up for the nights in question. A few car shapes went by. Henrik downloaded the images to his phone, and they were able to return to Jo's house as time was running out before the Packer game tailgate festivities. Kristy and Mike were also attending the game, so their conversation ended with the usual Green Bay salutation on game day of "Go Pack Go."

They had a few minutes before they needed to head to the stadium. The six of them would arrive in one vehicle, and Angela was walking over from her house. It was about a two-mile walk, but it was doable even on a cold day.

Henrik downloaded the images from his phone to a laptop and sent them off to his engineers for them to refine and send back to him. They would see if there was anything useable. At the end of the day, that might allow them to track down any suspects.

There was no response from the detective, so Jill assumed that he had no plans to share information with her. That wasn't surprising; she had run into that before with other cases. Or maybe he was there in the vast stadium parking lot tailgating prior to the game.

Soon they had the car packed for their tailgating adventure and cold weather game attendance. They arrived at the stadium and unloaded the cooler, table, and barbeque and were soon joined by Angela, who played bartender while Nathan cooked the meat. Then it was time to put everything away and make their way inside Lambeau Field.

After a military flyover at the end of the National Anthem, the game began. The Packers had already secured a playoff spot and with a win today could achieve the number one position, which would give them a week off to rest and recuperate. In the end, they went on to beat the Baltimore Ravens, and that gave them the number one seed. Around half time, Henrik's staff had refined the images to the degree they could, and they had the make, model, and color for any vehicles that arrived late at night. Of course, they couldn't tell what went on past Mike and Kristy's house due to the camera angle. Two of the vehicles were ruled out as neighbors who worked late shifts, but two other vehicles were something to follow up on.

They returned to their respective homes to continue their research on their own.

Henrik was able to look into the state vehicle registration system for the two unknown vehicles and retrieve information on their owners. There was only one trip made to the neighborhood on the estimated date the victims were placed in or near the house. This meant that if one of the vehicles was involved in the murders, then all of the bodies were dumped at the same time. Marie, Jo, and Jill went to work trying to find out what they could about each of the owners. They hit a wall when nothing looked suspicious from their review. Still, it would be good to know if any of the vehicles had been reported missing or had returned with perhaps a strange smell or stains. In the end, they ran down the vehicles and all were legitimately in the neighborhood, so that camera trail was at an end.

They had no more leads on the case, so they defaulted to their relaxing exercise of playing cards. Jill liked that she could compete with her friends in cards and in the back of her brain think about the case and develop additional clues. The case was eluding her at the moment, and she had no tips to follow up on. She decided to go back to the victims and look for some intersecting interests or connections between them.

Thinking back to the autopsy, the murder weapon offered no clue other than the murderer had come at the victims' chests first, and there were few defensive wounds. Were they stabbed in their sleep? They weren't sedated, so why didn't the victims fight back? Perhaps they were murdered in their homes and were moved to this location, but even that was a weird idea as someone would find their loved one missing and a pool of blood in an empty bed. She really wished the detective would talk with her. Maybe tomorrow she would take the rental car around to the houses and see if she could snoop into their living spaces. On that thought, and as the card game ended, she said good night to everyone as she mentioned she was going to explore the victims' homes the next day. Marie called out with an offer to help and they agreed to connect in the morning.

CHAPTER 6

The next morning brought no communication from the detective, so Jill planned a meetup with Marie to check out the houses. Henrik was using the time alone at Marie's house to get some work done. The two women set off to the first victim's house.

After putting the coordinates into Jill's GPS, Marie explained, "This is victim number one from the van. His name is Casey Gepson, a 45-year-old divorced father of three. He lives alone in the city of Pulaski and works for one of the local paper mills. Seems to love life and his kids. He has no criminal record. His ex-wife lives in the same city, and they appear to have amicably divorced and share custody of their kids. They are all devastated at the loss of Casey. They began posting on social media yesterday, though the police have not confirmed his identity yet."

"Yeah, they're usually in no hurry to announce

names. I wonder if there will be police tape around the outside of the house, as surely they were here yesterday collecting evidence."

They made the turn onto the street and Jill was pleased to see the detective's car parked out front. Maybe she could barge her way inside.

"That's Detective Van Lanen's car so it's up to us to talk our way inside to gain more clues or to pick his brain. Let's see how good we are at doing that," Jill said, reaching across the seats to fist-bump with Marie.

They got out and approached the house. Jill called out, "Detective Van Lanen, it's Dr. Jill Quint. May I come in? I know this is the residence of the first victim, Casey Gepson."

Jill stood in front of the door on the porch waiting for a response. Eventually, she heard someone approach and was surprised to see what was likely another police detective wearing latex gloves and booties over her shoes.

"Who are you? This is a crime scene. You cannot enter," the woman said.

Jill held out her credentials, identifying her as a licensed physician in pathology, as well as her PI license.

"Hi, I thought that was Detective Van Lanen's car. I worked with him two days ago to retrieve the five bodies from the murder scene in the Town of Scott. I also signed on as the Medical Examiner as your regular pathologist is on vacation. So I did the five autopsies. I'm familiar with crime scenes as I've been to hundreds of them in both of my roles. I want to help solve the case; as the bodies were left in my best friend's neighborhood. I also have a knack for helping the police. You can check my references with the detective. May I come in?"

"Who is this person with you? I could stretch department rules and allow you into the crime scene as the medical examiner, but I can't have another civilian on the scene."

Jill thought that was a fair compromise and nodded. Marie was gone in a flash, back to the car as she never wanted to see an actual crime scene. Jill signed the visitor log, put on booties and gloves, and entered the home.

"How many detectives are on this case?"

"We've got reduced staffing over the holidays, so all of us are working this case given the number of victims. I'm Detective Claire Hagstrom, by the way. Why are you here? I thought you were visiting from California?" the detective said as she walked Jill through the house to the bedroom.

"I *am* here on vacation, but this happened in my friend's neighborhood, which is why I got involved in the first place. Then you folks needed an ME and I was on the scene and credentialed. That said, I've worked in more of a PI role in many states and internationally. So I also bring investigative skills in addition to medical expertise to the scene. My friends, who live in Green Bay, join me on many cases. Marie, who just went back to her car, is a social media maven

—she can find any secrets on anyone. Jo, whose house I'm staying at, acts like a forensic accountant and can follow the money anywhere. Angela uses photography and interview skills to find new information, and Henrik is the CEO of an international IT firm that has the best facial-recognition software in the world, which many police agencies have purchased from him. He was able to identify and run criminal searches on all your victims faster than your department could."

"That's quite a team you've assembled. Here is where we think Mr. Gepson was killed. As the ME, can you verify that the victim likely bled to death in his bed?" the detective asked.

"Yes, he would have died after he lost about 4 quarts of blood, and even though this is dried and congealed, I would guess this is where the stabbing occurred. I don't see any blood on the floor, so your perpetrator must have wrapped him up in something to avoid soiling the floor when he moved the body."

"That's helpful. It would be helpful to visit the other homes as well. We have a detective at each home doing a search, and I'll forward them a text that you'll be arriving to have you confirm the murder site."

"Thank you, Detective. Is there anything more I can do for you here?"

"I'm going to look for the murder weapon and the trail out of the house. Maybe the victim dripped something somewhere on their way out. I'll also be interviewing the neighbors, so I'll be here a while."

"The murder weapon is a serrated knife. Likely 7 to 9 inches in length."

"Thank you, Dr. Quint, you've been helpful."

Jill exited the house, and Marie drove them to the next four houses, where Jill went through the same process with each detective. She now knew what the victims had in common. They all lived alone, and they all had been murdered in their beds, likely at night. She would need to learn their work schedules to understand when they slept, but her assumption was that they slept at night. She took the contact information for each detective in hopes of getting more information out of them. She asked at the final three houses if there were any signs of a robbery, but the detectives had not uncovered any yet. The victims' wallets and purses were untouched, and Jill could attest that the minimal but valuable jewelry was left on the bodies that she had autopsied. She'd expected to run into Detective Van Lanen at one the murder sites, but he was apparently elsewhere following up clues.

Jill and Marie returned to her house, where Marie was cooking that night. Nathan, Jo, and Matthew were already there, and Angela was on her way. Henrik was pouring wine after handling his business calls. The next day was Christmas, and they would each spend it with their families while Jill and Nathan would hang out with Jo's extended family. They were leaving in three days and were running out of time to find the murderer.

Jill recapped the highlights of what she had seen at

the murder scenes, including what the victims had in common. Marie had been doing searches from her car as she waited for Jill at each scene and had new information to share, but for now she was involved with cooking the dinner. Jill was dying to have Nathan take over cooking the meal so she could have Marie's information and help, but she knew that was a line not to cross with her friends when they volunteered to help with these investigations.

She patiently waited through dinner and dessert and then heaved a sigh of relief when they returned to the case. Jo had also done more investigation into the five victims.

Finally, she was able to begin firing questions at her friends. "Were all of the victims divorced? Why were they living alone? The first victim, Casey Gepson, sometimes had his kids over with him based on what I saw in the bedrooms of his house. So while he lived alone, he wasn't alone when his kids came for a sleepover. How did the killer know to strike when the kids weren't home?"

"It was easy to find through his social media posts. He posted pictures of his kids every other weekend and every Wednesday. So I think the killer either got lucky or he researched his victims to know when they would be alone."

"Was he dating anyone?" Jo asked.

"Not at the time of the murder. His divorce was finalized a year ago and I didn't see mention of a girlfriend since that time," Marie said

"Okay, next up is Crystal Seger. She's forty-four and never married. She's an aunt to her brother's three daughters. There was evidence at her house that she occasionally hosted her nieces," Jill said. "For a variety of reasons, we don't have an exact time of death, but after the police interview friends and family, it should narrow the window of time. What also struck me about these victims' homes was that they were not isolated—they were in blocks with other houses around. That reminds me that I should canvass those other homes and look for vehicles much like we did for Jo's neighborhood."

"This entire case has been done in a fairly public manner, and that's saying something given all of the remote houses in nearby communities to Green Bay. Let me look again at the victims' social media pages and evaluate if they were all open with their lives and if there is a commonality in friends or commenters," Marie said.

"And I'll ask some of my hackers if they can analyze visitors to their social media pages and, specifically, IP addresses," Henrik said, typing away on his phone.

"I should apologize for taking up your vacation time with us and Marie with this case," Jill said. "I feel bad that we're not doing something fun with this group."

"Ah, but you're selling my product to a new law enforcement agency, and by listening to this conversation, I'm thinking of an add-on to my software package to help solve crime. Listening to this group problem-solve is better than a paid focus group of law enforcement professionals. Jill, you're obsessed with solving these cases and bringing justice to the victims and their families like you did for me. I'm obsessed with making my software better every day so that worldwide you don't have to be on every case with your friends to solve it."

Those were such kind words that Jill had to get out of her chair and give Henrik a hug.

"Okay, I'm new to your process and cases and I've only seen murders solved on television in a half-hour segment, so this feels slow to me," Matthew said. Jo had lost her former partner during the Covid epidemic and he had been a wizard with video editing. Matthew, an accountant and her new partner, might be able to help Jo look at finances if he wanted to contribute to the group.

"There's a link among these victims that we haven't found yet. If we look back to all the cases we have solved, for the most part it has been about greed or jealousy. So you and Jo play a key role in searching through financial records to find where money might be a motivator. All of our victims seem to be regular Janes or Joes—no one was wealthy or poor. They were going about their lives. Dig deep into that; maybe these victims gambled, or played with cryptocurrency, or used loans to make ends meet, or screwed a prior partner at the time of a breakup," Jill suggested.

Matthew nodded and said, "Let me get my computer and compare notes with Jo. I'll see what her financial analysis process is and if I know any new avenues beyond the investigative route she's already taken."

"We're running out of time, and tomorrow is lost to most of the investigation because it's Christmas and rightly everyone will be with family, but keep me informed throughout the day if you think of something or discover something," Jill said.

The group broke up shortly after that, turning the page to the excitement of sharing Christmas with their families. Angela would be heading out to Midnight Mass, while everyone else was heading home to their respective beds. They were all in their late forties and there were a few young grandkids of Jo and Marie's to share the excitement of Christmas with the next day, but mostly it was about food, family, and good cheer. There were cookies to be distributed and a short volunteer stint at the local food bank.

CHAPTER 7

The next morning, Jill was up first with Matthew following to meet the demands of a hungry and vocal Diaper Boy and Beast. Jo's family would begin arriving around noon, with Christmas dinner being served around three in the afternoon. She was typing away on her computer, trying to find the link among the victims. She had made friends with the detectives at each murder site, but they saw her usefulness to them ending with confirmation of the murder site. They weren't into sharing any new information with her. Granted, she hadn't shared the video from the neighbor's bird camera feed, but the jury was still out regarding its usefulness. She sent a note to Henrik to see what his team had refined.

She also pulled up a map of the murder sites and plotted them visually. She sent it to Henrik wondering if his teenage hackers could find door cameras around the houses that they could access for footage of car traffic. Finally, she shut down her computer and looked out on the cold Green Bay water. Waves were crashing onto the shore, and there looked to be perhaps a 10 mph wind. There was a large ship coming into port escorted by a tugboat. There were virtually no other boats that she could see as Christmas morning was generally not a day for fishing. It was a quiet neighborhood on a quiet day.

She was back to thinking about the vacant house. Surely, the person who had dumped the bodies there knew they would be discovered at some point. Yes, the property was unoccupied, but it wouldn't stay that way forever. So Jill concluded that they wanted the bodies to be discovered. Why?

Why would the murderer want their crime discovered? It wasn't because of the victims; as they never would have murdered them to begin with if they had any compassion. Maybe the murderer thought they would gain notoriety once the bodies were discovered. Maybe they thought they would be reduced to bones by the time they were discovered, as no one would tear down the house in the winter, and by March or April, there would have been significant decomposition. The pipes' breaking in the basement was random. Who would have known that the family forgot to turn off the water after their father died, especially when the house made it through the first winter unscathed?

Why murder all of these people so close together in time? What was the order of placement in the boat, van, and basement? How did the murderer get into the van —was it unlocked, or had a window been broken? She hadn't noticed. Maybe she would take a walk over to the house now and look at the scene again to see if it gave her any clues.

Jill put on her snow boots, a long parka, gloves, and a hat, and she wrapped a scarf around her face. With the wind chill, it was in the single digits outside. She took her phone to record anything of interest and walked over to the deserted house.

The house was sadly desolate with crime scene tape around it, which was dumb in Jill's mind, as what neighborhood kid could resist the temptation of exploring a notorious murder scene? She approached the boat first. There had been a cover over it at one time, but sun, snow, and ice had broken down the plastic covering in the center. It would have been easy to dump bodies on the floor of the small boat. She judged that even at her height of 5'3", she could heave a body from her shoulder onto the boat floor.

Next, she moved onto the van. There were no broken windows, but the doors were unlocked. In many California locations, the boat and van would have been stolen long ago; and if they were not stolen, at least parts would be missing. People left abandoned things alone in Wisconsin. She popped the hood latch and saw an old battery in place. She took a picture of the door label to look it up later, but a catalytic converter or an airbag could have been removed and sold. She wondered why it was unlocked, but when she hit the lock button, the locks seemed to be stuck in the open position. Was that because the battery was long dead? Had the killer known that the van was unlocked before they targeted it as a dump site?

The only woman among the victims had been placed inside the van, and why was that? Why not put her in the basement where she also would have been protected from the elements? She was the lightest victim, so it would have been easier to move her the farthest distance. Jill thought back to the clothing covering the victims, and they all wore a variety of nightwear, though she hadn't necessarily recognized that at the time of the autopsy. Finally, she approached the house. The front door was locked and there was ice on the ground around the basement window where the authorities had first melted the ice, then pumped out the water. Given the weather conditions, that water had already refrozen outside the house.

Jill walked around the house looking for another door. She found one and walked up a few steps. There was an old notice on the door indicating that the power was cut off. She tried opening that door, and by putting her body weight against it, she was able to do so. She turned on her phone's flashlight app to see her way through the house. It was quite a sad little dwelling.

Jo had told her that it had no central heat and that the elderly gentleman had lived in two rooms that were heated through the winter. She could see a space heater and a fireplace. There was a small twin bed near the space heater. There was stuff everywhere, as though the family had made no effort to clear it out after his death. She was just walking around the corner to the basement when she heard the front door opening. She paused, wondering who would be here on Christmas morning. Should she stay quiet or call out?

She heard the intruder go down the steps toward the basement. Was the murderer back? Surely not. She tiptoed around the corner to peer at the intruder and was relieved to see Detective Van Lanen. What should she do now? Wait till he left, or admit that she invaded had his crime scene?

She gave a gentle knock on the door frame to announce her presence and called out, "Detective, it's Dr. Quint." No need to scare a man who likely carried a gun.

"This is a crime scene, Dr. Quint. What are you doing here?"

"Same thing as you are, trying to solve the case, or at least gain a clue about the suspect. I'm surprised to see you here Christmas morning. Aren't you off?"

"No, I'm on duty. My kids are older, so they've already awoken and opened presents. They're all in their bedrooms playing with their new stuff. We go over to my in-laws for dinner, so I'm taking some time to work on the case. Have you come up with anything new?"

"No, mostly new questions. Why were the victims distributed among the van, boat, and house? How did the murderer get into the house and van? I've got answers to those questions, but they don't put me any closer to identifying who the suspect is. Later, I'm expecting some more lab results to come in and maybe that will provide some new clues. How about you—what do you know about the case?"

"After interviewing friends and family, we think this murderous rampage took place over one night. This was a highly organized killer. They had to know each victim was asleep in bed alone, stab them, wait for them to bleed out, then move each of the five bodies into likely one vehicle and dump them here. There is some connection among these five people that we just haven't figured out yet."

"Yes, my team has searched social media for a connection, and we haven't found one yet, either. We know they were murdered in the same manner and that they were all single, either through divorce or had never married. Judging from the autopsy, the same knife was used on each victim. Did they start by slaughtering all five, then did they return to wrap them up and remove them from their homes? How did they know of the availability of the dump site? Either they worked for the Town or a utility company or he's somehow associated with a neighbor in this community. Also, he wanted the murders to be discovered at some point, but perhaps not as quickly as they were discovered. The water leak was unpredictable," Jill said

"So what else are you following up on?" the detective said.

Jill thought about additional leads and whether to share them with the detective. He might frown at some of the hacker activity—and it would be inadmissible in court—but he had at least shared with her that the murders had all occurred on the same night.

"I've told you a little about my team; as this is my friend's neighborhood and additional friends live in this region, we're not letting this drop. We surveyed this neighborhood for door cams and went through the footage for the house on the corner," Jill said, pointing to where Mary lived.

"What did you find? I haven't gotten that far yet."

"We looked at the four or five days when the body placement might have occurred and found nothing. However, that's not the only road into this neighborhood, and another neighbor had a bird camera on her feeder that aimed at the other entry street. The street footage is not great and my IT friend, Henrik, has had his staff perfect the images of the vehicles. We don't have license plates and have used AI to match the cars to their potential make and model. I'll send that to you."

"Thank you. That would be helpful."

"Next, I uploaded a map of the five murder sites, and my IT expert is having his staff check for neighboring houses that might have footage."

"How are they doing that? I'm not an IT expert, so I can't begin to guess."

"Let's just say that it might not be admissible in court, but you could use it to find the vehicle that transported the bodies and leave it at that."

The detective frowned at Jill, but then he thought of the time ticking by, the holidays, the pressure on the department to solve these murders, and the fear in the community including from his own wife about being murdered in one's bed while sleeping. The doctor was correct that they wouldn't likely need that specific piece of information for a court case, so if it was obtained illegally, he hoped he would be able to backfill with a legitimate way to find the vehicle.

"It's Christmas in Germany as well, so he has minimal staffing at his headquarters, but he has a few techy nerds who love a challenge like this no matter the day or time. Give me a minute to check my email and we may have some preliminary information."

Jill had shut down her flashlight app when she heard the intruder in the house and put the phone away. Now she pulled it out, took off her glove to open her screen and check. She shuffled through emails looking for something from Henrik. It was nearing the dinner hour in Germany and even the nerds likely had somewhere to be for Christmas dinner. She looked up and said, "Nothing yet, but he's never let me down, and I'll bet I have something by the end of the day. I do have the bird feeder images which I'll forward to you now."

"Thank you. I get the sense that if I told you to stay out of my investigation, you would ignore me. I've also had our department check your references, and all I've heard back was not to be an arrogant fool to try and exclude you from the case. I'm going to talk to my DA representative to see what information I can share with you in what manner by having you sign a particular piece of paper or maybe the original piece of paper will cover your actions here today."

"Thank you, Detective. I don't want to hamper your investigation, and I haven't when I've worked with other agencies in the past, but I also know that it's your nature to be leery of the skills of me and my team. I leave Wisconsin in another two days, and I would love to see you on television while I'm in the departure lounge announcing the arrest of the murderer. I want all the credit to go to you and your agency."

"I appreciate that, Dr. Quint, and I understand your desire and urgency to solve the case. Monitor your email and I'll see if I can get you more information. Is there anything specifically you want to know?"

"I'd like to see what you learned in talking with the friends and family of the victims. Were the victims concerned about anything in the lead-up to their demise? This was a well-orchestrated killing spree. The murderer knew that all the victims would be alone in their houses and asleep on their death date. That took some planning. These people were not randomly picked; they have something in common that we haven't figured out yet other than they were all single."

"Yes, I'm dumbfounded by the coincidence of their all being alone in their beds yet on different streets in different burbs in and around Green Bay. I haven't found the connection yet, nor have any of the other detectives. My captain is anxious to have some new information as there will be a press briefing later today."

"How about the local meth resident? We know he doesn't have an alibi, but could he be your killer as he knew about this vacant house?"

"I'm not sure he knew about the vacant house. He normally wouldn't have a reason to drive by it. Also, his intake at the jail shows a pre-existing bad back. He's not a big man and he's not muscle bound. I don't see someone in that condition moving five bodies from their homes to a vehicle and then to this location. He also lacks the planning gene; otherwise he wouldn't be going to jail as often as he does. So we continue to list him as a person of interest because that sounds better than we have no leads and no suspects."

"I don't envy the pressure your department is under, and yes, I agree it is not your local meth dealer, but could it be one of the visitors who pick up supplies from him?" Jill asked.

"That's a remote possibility, but like the dealer, those drug users also don't have a reason to drive down this street."

"That's true. What about other forensic evidence that you've collected at this scene and the victims' houses? Fingerprints, tire impressions, footprints, anything?"

"Fingerprint processing is slow as we have to rule out the victims and their family members. We haven't had any recent snow, so except for this location, there are no tire tracks. With the water leak here, the grounds so were trampled on by the time we came on the scene, the footprints are too messy to be of use."

Jill nodded, unsurprised.

"I've been trying to get inside the killer's head as this is such an odd case. The killings seem so random, but yet so planned. The killer could have dumped the bodies in a remote location. Why not just drive that single vehicle north and be done with it?"

"Yeah, we're not a big enough department to have a profiler, but I have put in a call to our local FBI office to see if we can get any resources there, but like everything else, they're low on staffing over Christmas. They will send us an expert tomorrow, but we're approaching 72 hours since discovery and a week since the actual murders. Now, I don't think the killer would have known about the pipe breaking scenario and would have thought that he had till spring to worry about discovery."

"Yes. Did any friends or family say anything that stuck with you?"

"I guess what stuck with me was how similar all of the victims were. They had no criminal records. They were liked by friends, family, and neighbors. They worked solid jobs. They lived alone and were attacked alone. I wonder if the killer had targeted perhaps ten people and went after the five he knew would be alone on this particular night. Was there a second person involved in these crimes?"

Jill nodded, unable to think of anything more to ask the detective while she had him in a talkative mood. So she said, "I'm going to head back to my friend's home now. Please send me the case files as soon as your legal eagles approve, and when I have information about vehicles on the streets around the houses, I'll send that to you."

They nodded to each other and Jill moved to leave before adding, "The back door isn't locked, and I didn't try to lock it from the inside. You might check that before you leave. There aren't many children who live in this neighborhood, but I could see them wanting to break in here."

He nodded and she turned to go.

CHAPTER 8

*J*ill made her way back to Jo's home, where everyone was now awake. She had been in the bone-chilling cold for almost an hour and just now realized that she could barely feel her feet and her eyes and nose were dripping. It was so cold that the tears froze on her cheeks before she made it indoors. She stood inside, still wrapped up until she began to warm up.

"Any new information? You were gone so long I was beginning to worry, but Nathan looked your location up on his phone and we could tell you were at the creepy house," Jo said.

"That's a good name for that house. It *is* creepy seeing how an elderly man lived his final years in the house. It's very cold and lonely. I managed to get inside the door at the top of the concrete stairs when I heard a sound outside and someone entered the house. Fortunately, it was the detective, so we had a long conversation. As you can imagine, his department is under pressure to come up with answers, and they are as clueless as we are. He was going to talk to his legal people to find a way to share their reports with us, which will include the interviews with people surrounding the murder victims. I told him I would share the car information that Henrik is working on as soon as we have it. They're trying to get a profile of the killer, but all of the people murdered were just nice Midwesterners. That's a scary demographic for a town like this."

"That's so sad. With my family coming, I'm committed to doing the set-up for dinner, so I can't help you at all today, but Matthew is looking into some things with the victims. So, there might be some new information coming from his searches in between barbecue duty."

"I wouldn't expect you to do any work today. Family comes first. Think of these five families that will be missing someone at the dinner table today. Gather your loved ones around you as none of us know how long we have on this earth," Jill said, and then she walked over to exchange a hug with Jo. "I would help you, but I'll let Nathan be your sous chef as he is so much more talented in the kitchen. I'll take my laptop to do some work downstairs for a few hours."

Jo nodded and Jill disappeared to the family room in the lower level of Jo's house. There were two bedrooms, a bathroom, and two large storage areas in her lower level. It was quiet now, so she could curl up with a blanket and her laptop and think about the victims. She reviewed the social media searches from Marie a couple of times. She continued to be struck by the fact that these victims were such average human beings.

The detective sent over some reports, and she received lab reports, surprising considering it was a holiday. She looked at them and found the one commonality among the victims—they were all diabetics. They had A1C lab tests in the diabetic range. An A1C test measured blood sugar over the long term, so it wasn't as if they all ate sweets just before they were murdered. So, either they didn't know they had the disease, or they were poorly managing their sugars. It was a strange factor to find in common, and it wasn't something that she had seen in any other murder case. Still, she passed on the information to the detective with some information about age group and incidence. Could the killer have met them in a diabetic education class?

Maybe the detective could go back and interview the families and ask about the diabetes. The police would certainly want to retrieve their medical records to see if they were followed by a doctor for the disease. Could she use her power as a medical examiner to request access to those records? In most states she could, but given her unlicensed status in this state, she dropped a detailed email to the Milwaukee ME to see if he would ask on her behalf.

Was there some insurance executive killing off people with expensive diabetes conditions? Or an endocrinologist tired of patients not listening to him? Or was this just a random piece of garbage information? None of her victims had been morbidly obese, which made sense in one manner as how would the killer move someone who weighed more than, say, 250 pounds?

She indicated in her email to the detective about her follow-up and the low likelihood that this weird factoid had anything to do with the case. He responded with interest, agreeing it was a strange factoid, but it was all they had at the moment for the single common denominator among this group of people.

She also received a response from the Milwaukee ME that he had access through IT to many of the health systems medical record software systems, and when he had a chance later that day, he would find out if their victims were being treated for the disease. Still, to Jill it was such a wild reason to kill five people that she couldn't believe that it had anything to do with it. She could see the headline now, *Diabetic Killer Arrested in Green Bay*, it would have police agencies snickering country wide, and diabetics living in fear.

She went back to the blood work to see if anything else showed up among the five, but there was nothing. She decided to move onto a new subject while she awaited the response of the Milwaukee ME. She went back to Marie's social media summaries to see if there were any mentions of dealing with diabetes, but apparently either the victims didn't know or didn't talk about their disease in their posts. Marie had a way to find out more information than Jill, but when Jill tried finding their social media accounts and searching for the word *diabetes*, it was a lost cause.

She looked at the time on her watch and called it quits. It was time to join the folks upstairs and share some holiday cheer. She heard more noise coming from the upper level and assumed it was Jo's sisters and her daughters arriving with their spouses. It was time to put work away and let her brain cogitate in the background. She logged out of the ME reports and took her laptop upstairs to her bedroom, where she put it away. The last thing she wanted was a child reviewing autopsy photos.

She spent the next few hours soaking up the holiday atmosphere and watching Jo's young grandchild being everything that the holidays are about. She recognized that she hadn't thought about the case for almost two hours that afternoon. How refreshing for her brain to step away from the case.

However, once the company was gone or in bed, her mind returned to the case at hand. Who had murdered five people and then dumped them in Jo's neighborhood? Did the fact that they were diabetics have anything to do with the case? On average, 11% of the population had diabetes, so in a town the size of Green Bay, that gave their killer 15,000 victims to choose from. When Jill examined the lab findings from that angle, it seemed random rather than the factor that made them the victim. She needed to find the intersections where these five people crossed. The fact that they were single was also not a unique circumstance as there were simply too many people who were single and living alone as the two terms weren't mutually exclusive.

When looking at people who committed crimes, the police narrow it down to means, motive, and opportunity. Living alone created the opportunity to get in, stab the victim, and wait for them to die, and then move the body to Jo's neighborhood.

If Jill looked at the means, then she focused on a male assailant as they had to be strong enough to move the dead weight, no pun intended, of the victims. How did they get inside the residence? She pulled up the police report to see if there was evidence of the killer's entry to the houses.

The killer must have been good at picking locks as there was no evidence that the houses were broken into. None of the houses had alarm systems, which was not unusual. So the killer or his accomplice had a lock-picking skill.

The houses were about ten to fifteen minutes apart, so what was the order of the murders? Go through and stab each person in the heart, then return later to wrap them up and move them? The first part could conceivably take place in under an hour. Then the killer needed a second hour to retrieve the bodies, and a third hour to drive them to their final resting spot.

Jill was pleased to see some information come in from Henrik's people. They had finalized their identity of the vehicles that passed the bird feeder camera.

Furthermore they had hacked into the cameras around the first two victims' houses and found a match for one of the vehicles. It was a dark-colored, relatively new pick-up truck.

Jill wondered about the vehicle. The first two victims would have been slid onto the pick-up's bed, but after that, the first two bodies would consume the space of the truck bed. The next three would need to be dumped over the side of the pick-up truck and onto another body already resting there. What a gruesome thought. A pickup truck made a fair amount of sense as it was easy to hose down or be taken through a car wash. As this was a hunting part of the country, people would naturally assume that it was a deer or bear's blood in the truck. Also, there would be no permanent staining of the metal surface. And as the victims were already dead, who cared if they were exposed to the cold air or snow?

Jill was beginning to feel like she was running in place with this investigation. Did she have any more leads now than she did at the beginning of the case?

She decided to give up and head to bed. Then she said goodnight to the assembled card-playing crowd answering a few questions on the way out like, "No, I don't know who the killer is."

She braided her long blond hair so she wouldn't roll on it in bed, and fell asleep trying to assemble a killer portrait of his likes and dislikes before sleep took over.

The next morning she was up early. There was new information from the detective as well as lab values for her to follow up on. Neither gave her particularly new information. Then she started writing down ideas for motives. Greed or financial issues, passion, jealousy, revenge, mentally ill, or simply the killer was truly evil. The randomness of the victims suggested that murder due to strong emotions was unlikely to be the motive, which left her with someone mentally ill or just pure evil.

What kind of mentally ill person murdered five people in so ruthless a fashion? Thinking back over decades of experience with murder victims, she couldn't think of a single mentally ill killer capable of planning and carrying out these five murders. Jill pulled out the pictures taken at the crime scene and looked at them, studying the bedrooms of the victims. Then something caught her attention. What was it about these pictures? There was something out of sync with each picture.

Then the thought came into focus as she switched back and forth between the crime scene pictures. There was a baseball trading card in each person's bedroom. So might the second thing they all had in common be a love of baseball? Jill didn't follow baseball, but she knew the season was over. The World Series had been back in October. The new season didn't start until March, she thought. The baseball cards weren't just from the local favorite—the Brewers. She looked the cards up to see if they were valuable. Of course, each of them had a smear of blood on it, so if they had been valuable, they weren't now.

She picked up her cell phone to make a call.

"Detective, I was just studying the crime scene photos, and did you notice each bedroom had a baseball trading card in your pictures?" Jill asked, once she got the polite greetings out of the way.

"Yeah, I noticed that this morning. I've sent someone to collect them and fingerprint them. It was odd that they all had one and they weren't just from the home team."

"I just checked the cards out and they're not valuable from a collector's perspective. I'll ask my team to find out if any of them were baseball fans," Jill said.

"Remember that some of the houses contained kids at times and they could have been collectors."

"True, but . . ."

"You don't like coincidences."

"Yes. Also, they all have blood on them and that's just beyond coincidence. It feels like those cards are talismans of the killer. That said, I don't think we'll be lucky enough to find fingerprints on them."

"No I don't see us being that lucky. By the way, we did a search for the pick-up truck that might be involved, but there are simply too many dark-colored trucks for the description to be a help," the detective said.

"Yeah, I sort of figured that would be your conclusion. I've been thinking about a motive for this killer, and I'm not coming up with anything. The fact that they were all diabetics and had baseball trading cards doesn't seem sufficiently passionate enough to cause this murder spree."

"I would agree with you."

"I also think this is too well planned for a mentally ill person to be the perpetrator. So that leaves me with someone who is just pure evil—a serial killer."

"We'll see what the FBI provides us with later today. Their crime profiler is supposed to render us with something."

They ended their call shortly after that, and Jill wondered what an expert psychological profile would say about the person who committed these murders. Then she thought of something to ask Henrik.

CHAPTER 9

The friends were gathering for dinner that evening, and then they would head out to see the Festival of Lights at the Botanical Garden. She dropped a note to Henrik with the five crime scene photos that included the baseball trading cards. She asked him to search the internet for copies of the pictures that might be posted somewhere. It was a long shot, but with so little information about the killer she would chase long shots.

Trying to put aside the current case, she rejoined Jo, Matthew and Nathan in the kitchen. She was ready for lunch and wanted to see what everyone else was up to.

"We're grabbing leftovers now and dinner is at six." Jo said, naming a restaurant that everyone was familiar with. All of Jill's friends were used to her focusing on a murder case instead of them whenever she was involved with a case.

Jill nodded and started filling her plate.

"What new clues have you found?"

"The truck that we isolated from the bird camera of your neighbors is too common to be useful."

"But. . . . I hear something in your voice that your curiosity has piqued," Jo said.

"There was a baseball trading card left at each murder scene. There is blood on each card, so it has no trading value, and even if it was in better condition, the cards don't have much value. The police are testing the cards for fingerprints and for blood to see if they match the victims. Some of the cards are for the Brewers; others are not. So the five victims now have three things in common: one, they had a baseball trading card in their bedroom; two, they were diabetics; and three, they were alone the night that they were murdered."

"Four: they worked the day shift, so they slept at night," Jo added.

"True that. I asked Henrik if his staff could search the web to see if there were any pictures of the crime scene posted in the darkest corner of the internet. I was chatting with the detective earlier, and from a motive perspective, nothing makes sense except a serial killer who is pure evil."

"Wow. Have we had any other cases of the perps being pure evil." Jo asked.

"We've had a few. Remember the woman who was cleaning up the dating pool as an arsonist? Or our most recent case with killing senior citizens in order to clear mobile home parks for housing tracts?"

"I agree with you on the arsonist, but I would argue the guy who murdered the seniors had greed as a motivation. I think most serial killers are just pure evil. Sure, there's some mental illness mixed in, but at the base of it all is just evil beyond my understanding."

"It's sad to think about those five families missing someone at their table during this holiday season," Matthew said.

"Yes, it is. They won't ever again be at the holiday table. There are children missing a parent or an aunt from this date forward. I guess the only positive spin I could put on this is that at least the killer disposed of the bodies in a manner that we found them. Imagine not knowing why Aunt Mary never showed up for Christmas dinner. I guess there is no good outcome to this terrible situation," Jill said with a sigh. She would admit to herself that it was sad dealing with murder over the holiday season.

"Are you planning to work some more on the case this afternoon?" Nathan asked.

"No. I've done everything I could with it. Why, what do you have planned?"

"How about a game of pickleball with our hosts?"

"I could do that. In fact, swinging a paddle against the pickleball might ease my tension from the frantic need to solve this case before we leave."

"Excellent!" Matthew said. "I'll go make a court reservation for about an hour from now."

They sat down to eat, talking about friends, family, and the holiday. Jo invited Henrik and Marie to join them for the scheduled game later. Even though the numbers would be uneven, they could rotate in and out and still have a great time.

By the time they arrived at the indoor pickleball courts, Henrik had some news to share with Jill. His niece, who was the best at finding stuff in the dark corners of the internet, had indeed found pictures of trading cards posted.

Jill was tempted to go right to work and find out who and what they were posting, but she didn't want to spoil everyone's holiday celebration with talk of murder. Instead, she concentrated on killing each and every ball that flew her way. Nathan had to whisper to her at one point that she should cool her jets as she was being too aggressive and not fun to play with. With that advice, she did soften her swings at the ball.

They finished and were walking out when Henrik said, "Remind me never to play this game with you in the middle of one of your murder cases. I almost ended up being one of your bodies on a stainless-steel table."

"Oh come on, I wasn't that bad, was I?," she asked, looking at Jo and Marie.

"Ah, you really were that bad," Jo and Marie nodded together.

"Sorry, guys. I feel like I'm under pressure to get this case solved before I leave since it is in your neighborhood, Jo."

"Don't worry about it. I'm sure the police will eventually solve it, and think of how you've accelerated their progress between the autopsies, the web cams, and Henrik's search of the dark corners of the internet."

"That's true. You guys know me, though. I like to have a case resolved before I leave town, and I feel a little more invested than usual because it happened so close to your house."

"Yes, but let's head home and shower and get ready for dinner and a nighttime walk at the botanical gardens light show. What would you have done with your time if you hadn't had this case to work on?" Marie asked.

"That's a good question. I've been to Green Bay several times in the past, and I haven't had an active case. I'll try and take a chill pill and just enjoy the company of my friends, the food, and later the lights."

All of Jill's friends froze and looked at her.

"What? You don't think I can take a chill pill?"

"We know you can't and we still love you anyway."

"I know, friends. Thanks for putting up with me."

"Nathan, how do you put up with your wife's focus on murder?" Henrik asked with amusement in his voice.

"It was part of the package I married. I knew she could go off at any moment and try to solve a murder. In fact, she did so shortly after our wedding ceremony, if you all remember."

"Only because we found our officiant dead. Otherwise, our wedding would have been free and clear of murder."

"As much as I would harass you about turning our

wedding night into a murder investigation, you did the right thing in finding her killer."

"Yes, and that is what I'm trying to do with these five victims. While it won't get them back to their dining room table at Christmas, at least the families will have some resolution."

"Is there anything we can do beyond the research we already did?" Marie asked.

"You could look into the baseball trading cards to see if that was important to the lives of the victims or their families."

"I can do that. Give me an hour and I'll have an answer for you."

"Jo and Matthew, would you look at their financial records to see if they were into buying and selling baseball trading cards? I don't think they were, but I could close that loop with a little research on your part. As Marie's house is closer, maybe we could stop there so that everyone can do a little research in private."

They nodded and soon were organized in Marie's living room working on their phones. A short time later, she had her answer that there was no history of buying or selling trading cards from any sport. Meanwhile, Marie noted that two of the victims were uninterested in baseball and the other three had a mild interest as evidenced by mentioning a baseball team at least once on the social media page over the past five years. Three of them had young children who had played T-ball or softball. Marie also added that one of the five did some sports betting.

Darn, this wasn't helping her understand a motive for the deaths and thus identifying a suspect. Henrik forwarded the links from his niece, and Jill studied those pictures. She kept looking back and forth to determine if there were any differences in the pictures. The ones on the internet were taken from a different angle than the police images. The cards did have a splatter of blood on them, but it hadn't dried yet, so the shade of red was lighter. The houses were untouched for up to 72 hours after each victim's murder, which was plenty of time for blood to dry on the cards before the police photos were taken. She was looking at images taken by the killer, and it was shocking.

She dialed Detective Van Lanen. When he answered, she said, "I have some really weird evidence. My friends were able to find crime scene photos on the internet. I'm guessing that the killer took them as it looks like the blood is not yet dried on the baseball trading cards in this version."

"Wow! I think I better see those photos as soon as possible and I'll need to talk with your friend as to where he or she found them."

Jill sent one of the photos to the detective. After a moment, he said, "I see what you mean. What's the physical location of you and your friends at the moment? I need to understand where these photos were found."

She gave the detective Marie's address, and after she ended the call informed them all that the detective was on his way over. Henrik texted his niece in Stuttgart to be available for an interview with the American police.

Jill looked at the time, and they had a few hours before their dinner reservation. Meanwhile, she also wanted to speak to Henrik's niece to understand where she found the pictures. Jill had met his niece during past cases. She had been able to unlock phones and do all kinds of sketchy techy things. As good as Henrik was with technology and IT systems, his niece was in an entirely different brainiac level.

Henrik was consulting with his legal eagles to make sure his niece was not at risk for anything she revealed. In the interim and until the detective arrived, Jill wanted to speak with her.

"Hello, Lea."

"Hello, Dr. Quint."

"It's Jill. I feel with all the work we've done together to find criminals we should be on a first-name basis. I assume your uncle texted you that the American police want to chat with you about where you found the photos online, and I thought I would get a head start. Tell me about your process. Did you upload the crime scene photos and then ask your computer to find a match?"

"Think Uncle Henrik's face-scan app, but leveled up for objects instead of people. We're stress-testing it at work—early beta stuff, not public yet—but your pics were a killer test run."

"Wow. I can imagine that would be helpful in all

kinds of areas. Weapons identification, physical locations, and things like that."

"Yeah, exactly! Seven billion faces were already a nightmare. Now toss in every random street, couch, and coffee mug on the internet—it's like trying to beat a game with infinite levels," Lea said.

"Wow. I now understand how difficult this must be. I guess we're lucky we got a match on the photo."

"Good news—our system isn't just searching for 'baseball card.' I basically told it, 'yo, grab everything in this pic—the table, the shadows, the card, the blood— and find *that exact scene.*' It's like face ID, but instead of eyes and noses, it's spotting a blood-smeared trading card chilling in the dark."

"Got it. So where exactly did you find a match?" Jill was amused when Lea let her guard down and spoke with her as if Jill knew about computers and games and software.

"Do you know what role-playing games are?"

"Yes. I don't play myself, but I actually read some books that are role-playing game stories."

"Yes, well it's a huge and ugly area of the internet. The line between reality and fantasy is hard to define. So you have creators adding content and interacting with fans. Because everyone is in the midst of a game, you can't tell when a player has stopped knowing this is a game and when they take on the mental attitude that it's all real. Then you get people acting stupid, believing the game they are playing is real."

"Yikes. There have been a couple of cases here in the

States where crimes were committed because the player couldn't differentiate between the online game and the real world."

"Yes. I think that might be what's going on with the photo you sent me. I think that because of where I found the photo. It was inside a video game called Murder-Rage."

Henrik walked over to where Jill was talking to his niece and said, "You can say whatever you want to the detective when he speaks with you in a bit. Our legal counsel has you protected."

"Thank you, Uncle Henrik," Lea said. They had a special relationship as she was the one relative who had the most potential to take his company to new heights. Among his generation, he'd been the genius with computers, but his niece was taking it to an entirely new level at the young age of twenty-two. She was that rare combination of brains, common sense, and fun. Lea was definitely his favorite relative.

"Did I hear you mention a game?" Henrik asked.

"Yeah, the Murder-Rage game is hiding out in a sketchy corner of the internet since it got banned in, like, half the world. I spotted the crime scene pics dropped in a sub tied to it—total dark-web creepy vibes. It's got these glitchy, flashing visuals—like walking through a haunted house built by someone who hates sleep. The chats are full of emojis and messed-up gore jokes. People are literally arguing about which kill methods should earn faster level-ups, like it's some twisted RPG. And the usernames? Total nightmare fuel—*ThroatSlasher*, *DeathBy1000Cuts*, even *Blood-yMary*, who straight-up pretends to drink her victims' blood."

Jill had found many video games violent, and she wondered what was so bad about this game that it was banned in multiple countries. This game was perhaps the most repulsive she had ever heard of. She felt bad that Lea even had to view it.

"Henrik, tell me about this banned video game. I assume it was banned, based on what Lea just described. Does banning work, or does it just retreat to a dark corner? Also, how can we protect your staff, including Lea, from these horrific online images? I want to vomit just thinking about some crazy fool who wants to drink other humans' blood."

"For the most part, banning doesn't work unless you live in a state-controlled country. People find illegal games, gambling, child porn, and other illegal and immoral stuff if they look far enough into the dark holes of the internet. As for my staff, they have seen horrific things working for my firm. I support them with an on-site psychologist and rotate them away from these terrible sites. In this case, Lea is pretty good at limiting her actual viewing of stuff as the software provides a summary of the images, rather than her having to look at the images and describe them herself. It's one of the reasons my company is working on this new software; we want to reduce the exposure of such horrific images by law enforcement. Imagine what viewing child porn does to your soul over time."

"Why was the game banned? Do you know if it's banned in the United States?"

"It is banned in your country and none of the app stores sell it, but sick people can always find a way to its location. It was banned for excessive violence. It runs like a crappy horror movie, but in at least one country, the game and reality have proved to be the same, with someone dying in a horrific way."

"That's sick. How does the game stay around and how is it monetized? Doesn't the creator need money to build and upgrade the app?" Jill asked.

They heard a doorbell ring and assumed it was the detective arriving so they paused their conversation.

CHAPTER 10

*M*arie welcomed Detective Van Lanen and another detective whose name Jill didn't remember, although he had been at one of the crime scenes. Detective Van Lanen introduced him as Detective Church.

"Detectives, meet Henrik Klein. He owns the facial-recognition company I mentioned. He's a citizen of Germany and is here on vacation. His niece Lea is on the video call and she is presently in Germany. We were just discussing a horrible-sounding role-playing game called Murder-Rage. Henrik, why don't you and Lea describe the game and why it is banned in most countries of the world?"

Henrik explained the rumors about the game, stating that he and his niece had never actually played the game to confirm what they had heard about it.

"So, Mr. Klein, your employee, who happens to also

be your niece, found our crime scene pictures in the corner of the internet where people are playing the game or talking about or hosting it?" Detective Van Lanen was furiously writing down details as Henrik and Lea explained them.

"Detective, have you played any of the popular role-playing games from Dungeons and Dragons, to Grand Theft Auto, to the World of Warcraft?" Henrik asked.

"Yes, I've played some of those games. Are you saying our crime scene photos ended up in the middle of a game?"

"Yes. It's not clear yet who posted them or why they were uploaded. We think the baseball cards may be proof tokens. There could be a range of reasons for this to happen," Henrik said.

"Such as?" the detective asked.

"Perhaps the players gain game points if they upload crime scene pictures. That would imply that the gamer was either at the scene of the crime or hacked into your law enforcement database."

"What would be among other awful reasons that this website might have those pictures?"

"One of the reasons this game was banned in so many countries was that it was believed to entice players into carrying out an actual murder, supply proof tokens, and gain points in its online community so they could level up."

There was shocked silence in the room at that pronouncement. *Someone would murder five people in reality in order to level up in a video game? What a horrible game for someone to have invented.* No wonder it was banned.

"Henrik, is there a way to take this off the internet, or will it always exist in the darkest corners?" Marie asked.

Jill looked around at her team, the detectives, Henrik, and even Lea, on the video screen, all had a look of shocked disbelief that someone could invent something so evil and that people would play such a game.

"If you can find the inventor of the app, you could probably get it removed, but like other nasty things of the internet, it's very difficult."

"So are you saying our killer is playing a game that kills real people?" asked Detective Church in disbelief.

"I'm not saying that just yet. I'm filling in the back-story about this role-playing game and giving you the location of your crime scene photos," Henrik said cautiously.

"Can you or Lea hack into this game app to see who the developer is and if he or she directed our killer to kill these five people to level up in the game?" Jill asked.

"Not yet. It's well protected and we can't work mira-cles, but we can do more research. We've just scratched the surface here. I wouldn't be surprised to find this game sitting in a country that is an enemy of the United States because someone is manipulating someone in your town to kill people. In my experience, some game designers are psychopaths and do it for the thrill of watching someone else follow their orders. It's just that these orders are terrible and sow chaos. Remember, we are just at the tip of the iceberg in discovering information about this game."

"We need to talk to some people in our department and in the FBI. We initially called them as it looked like we had a serial killer on our hands. Now we need their computer resources to help identify the developer, as you called him or her, and the gamer who carried out their orders," Detective Church said.

"How much longer are you visiting the United States, Mr. Klein?" Detective Van Lanen asked.

"I'm due to return to Germany on an overnight flight tomorrow. Both Lea and I will continue to work on this case, and we will assist you remotely from Germany. On our end, this is about computers and the internet and we could be anywhere in the world and still assist with the case."

Marie moved closer to whisper something in Henrik's ear, and they stepped outside to finish their conversation. The two detectives looked suspicious. The couple returned a short time later and Henrik said, "My friend, Marie, has reminded me that I can run my company from anywhere in the world and I need to stay here and assist you anyway that I can, so I will follow her request. We want to make Jo's neighborhood safe again."

The detectives' shoulders relaxed a little at this piece of news. This was a technologically complicated case, and they liked having the expert on hand rather than half a world and many time zones away.

"Do you think the gamemaster has more murders planned?" Nathan asked.

"Probably, though not necessarily in this city. Remember, this is a worldwide game that is being played, and the goal for any gamer is to level up. We're going to have to do a deep dive into the game and see what has already happened," Henrik said. "This is not my company's area of expertise, but I've got people who can dig into it along with your computer resources," he said to the group.

The detectives looked at each other, clearly blanking on any computer resources that their department had to investigate such an unusual case.

"Our department has detectives trained to do basic social media, porn, and financial searches, but what you're talking about is far beyond our skill set. The FBI is joining the case today, and I think I'd better call my contact there as this changes the profile of the killer; perhaps they have some teenage hackers who can search the dark corners of the web for our suspect and his or her gamemaster," Detective Van Lanen said.

"We're heading out to dinner soon. Maybe we could set up a time early tomorrow morning to meet at your headquarters to discuss strategy with the case," Henrik suggested. "That will give you the remainder of the day to brief your FBI and get the appropriate resources from them lined up."

The two detectives still looked stunned at the direction the case was going. This was not at all what they had discussed or examined while studying for their law enforcement degrees. They also owned video game consoles in their homes and knew that their children played role playing video games. They needed to do a deeper study of what was involved in the games to make sure their children were safe and they weren't unduly influenced by a game or gamemaster. They also needed to brief their lieutenant and likely the chief.

"We have other stuff to review as well—how did the killer know about the place where he dumped the bodies? And why choose to dump bodies where they'll be discovered versus dumping them in the woods where they might never be discovered?" Jill asked. "Beyond loads of computer work, there is much more to do on this case. I think because most of us don't understand the foundation of the internet and how it works, we see that as the barrier to solving this case. In reality, we need to understand why the bodies were placed where they were, as that may also help us find the killer."

Shortly after Jill's statement, the meeting broke up with Jo, Matthew, Nathan and Jill heading to Jo's house to change their clothes for their dinner, while the detectives planned to head to the station to talk with a variety of people about the computer issues in this case.

When the friends met up for dinner, they updated Angela about their latest discoveries and their next steps.

"Wow, role playing games result in the deaths of five people. What's wrong with this world?"

"There's mental illness everywhere. I'll bet that the

gamemaster is a psychopath and the actual killer who kills to please the gamemaster has their own array of issues," Jill said.

The entire table nodded at Jill's comment. She wasn't a psychiatrist, but she'd be the first to admit that it didn't take a genius to come to that conclusion about the killer.

"What can I do to help?" Angela asked. "I don't know anything about video games, but . . ."

Jill thought about Angela's skills with interviewing people and with a camera.

"It would be interesting to have you walk Jo's neighborhood to see if you can locate any other door or bird cameras. We have the likely vehicle that the killer drove, but we don't have a clear view of the make and model, or the license plate. It's too common a vehicle to do anything with it."

"Let me have my staff look at the bird camera to see if the blurry vehicle was spotted in the neighborhood over the past month," Henrik said. "Wouldn't you agree, Jill, that the killer wouldn't have driven around with a truck filled with five dead bodies looking for a place to dump them and just happened upon the house in Jo's neighborhood? The killer had to have scouted the dump site before he killed these people?"

"I agree with you, Henrik, that the killer had to know about the vacant house in advance. The timeline was too tight for someone to murder five people, then go back and pick up their bodies, and then search this city for a vacant house. In the middle of the night, many houses are dark, so how would you even find an empty house? The killer definitely knew about the house ahead of time. So then the question becomes, will we spot the same vehicle in Jo's neighborhood over the previous weeks and months, or did he use a different vehicle for this job? Also, let's look for the vehicle this week after the bodies were dumped. Could he live in this neighborhood, or is he a frequent visitor?"

Henrik nodded and typed something into his phone and the conversation moved on.

"How was everyone's Christmas? Did Santa think you were naughty or nice?" Nathan asked. He was great at heading the conversation in a new direction.

The group discussed children and grandchildren reactions to Christmas. Jo's two daughters and grand-daughter and Marie's son, two daughters and two grandkids were all pleased with their Christmas. After lingering over dessert and wine, they left with the promise to meet at Jo's house early the next day. It would be the day of the big push for new information as Jill and Nathan were scheduled to leave the day after.

Jill could delay their departure if there was a reason to stay nearby, but off the top of her head the only advantage of being in Green Bay to solve this murder was physical access to the detectives. Otherwise, she could do everything from her vineyard in California. Nathan could stay another day or two as well, as he had taken a break from work and had no new wine label designs that were due between Christmas and New Years.

They played a game of 313 rummy, and then Jill went to bed as she would be up early the next day. Matthew, Jo, and Nathan were chatting about a variety of things. The Northern Lights were rumored to be clear close to midnight that night, so they were planning on going outside in the cold later that night to look at the northern sky. Jill drifted off thinking about the two big puzzles of this case—how did the killer find the house and what makes an individual so lose touch with reality that he would find himself killing real people in order to level up in a role-playing game? She'd seen some dumb reasons to commit murder, but this might take the cake in its senselessness.

Angela arrived before Jo was awake the next morning, and she and Jill set out to examine the neighborhood homes for additional cameras, whether wildlife or security. The neighborhood had two streets that ran north-south and three streets that ran east-west. From what Jill could observe, the farther north-south street (the one to the east) had double the traffic of the other. Someone arriving from metro Green Bay would take the first street, so the killer should have taken that street to reach their dump site as it was the closest route to the deserted blue house.

So why didn't the killer do that? The only reason Jill could think of was that the killer had visited one of the ten or so houses, so the farther north-south street made sense to turn on for the shortest distance to a house. She commented on that piece of logic to Angela, who shrugged and said Wisconsin people were creatures of habit.

They discussed their script as they walked to the farthest neighbor on the street. Angela would take the lead and Jill would just listen and take notes. The vast majority of the neighbors had heard of the murders and were quick to point out any cameras they had that faced the streets. Also, every neighbor pointed to the meth house as the likely culprit. Most of the neighbors were disappointed to hear that it likely wasn't their meth neighbor as he did not appear to be strong enough to carry out the physical parts of these murders.

Two hours later, they had met most of the neighbors and had sent footage to Angela's email, for her to forward on to Henrik or a security camera company name if they didn't know how to get old files from their system. Jill had every hope that Henrik and his people would be able to hack into these systems to gather any footage. Once they got back to Jo's house, everyone was awake, and Marie and Henrik had arrived. They looked through the footage that was sent to them, and Henrik's hackers went to work on the other systems.

In the end, they found the truck on other cameras. They still didn't have a license plate but they now had a make and model. Jill forwarded the information to the detective, but she already knew that there were hundreds of pick-up trucks of that make, model, and color. Next she set about searching for the truck entering the neighborhood over the past two months.

Unfortunately, most of the doorbell camera subscriptions held onto video footage for just two weeks, and then it was discarded. The murders occurred about a week ago, so she was looking in just that narrow period of time of about a week before the murders.

Meanwhile, Henrik had his best hackers trying to break through the ugly corner of the dark web where the game Murder-Rage was hosted. So far they hadn't been successful at breaking into the game. His staff had tried joining as new players, but they hadn't been able to yet. His teenage hackers were giving it one more try to become players, then they planned to hack into another player's account to join the game. Jill wondered if they would find other murders from other players who had leveled up. It was quite an evil- game.

Fortunately, Henrik's team was able to hack into parts of the game, and there were different names for each level. Jill examined the list of level names with disgust: Clumsy Killer, Knife Enthusiast, Body Collector, Murderlord, Silent Stalker, Master of Knives, Overachieving Serialist, and Hall of Infamy Inductee.

What level had their killer achieved by killing five people? For the safety of the greater world, she hoped that their murders were the final level of Hall of Infamy Inductee. She was worried that it might have been for Knife Enthusiast as each of the victims had been murdered by a knife to the heart. If this is what the killer did at level 2, what unimaginable horror do they have in store for the world at the top level?

Jo's doorbell rang and it was the detectives along

with several people wearing dark blue jackets saying *FBI* on them. She invited them inside to a crowded living room. Introductions were made, and Jill was pleased to note that the FBI group included a computer expert in addition to what she assumed was their normal personnel response. The computer expert was soon speaking geek to Henrik and Lea. Eventually, every other conversation stopped to listen to the computer discussion. It was the heart of the case. It contained the motive and the identity of the killer and the gamemaster. Nothing else seemed relevant to the case—not the autopsy results, nor the identity of the victims and their backgrounds, nor anything thus far from the scene.

From their effort of speaking to the neighbors that morning, Jill and Angela had collected a few more cameras to look at. Fortunately, someone inside Henrik's company was reviewing those cameras. It would have taken Jill ages to examine the footage. Instead, his people gave them a list of dates and times where they saw the pick-up truck that they think was used to transport the bodies. The license plates had been removed so there was nothing to identify the vehicle. Still, given the frequency that the truck was in the neighborhood, the vehicle's driver either knew someone in the area or had worked on a project there. The vehicle was there both in daylight and in the evening. Since the bodies had been placed in the vacant house, there were no more sightings of the vehicle.

So did the killer sell or otherwise dispose of the

vehicle, or did they use it for the month surrounding the murder because they rented the truck? Maybe that was another question to ask the neighbors—who has had construction projects, landscaping, tree removal, or repairs that might have had strange vehicles in this isolated neighborhood? Perhaps if they tracked the times the vehicle appeared on the tape, they would find a connection to a job or resident.

Jill tuned back into Geeksville to see if Henrik and Lea were making progress. From the sound of it, they were trading rapid-fire suggestions with the FBI dude, trying different things to get into the Murder-Rage game. They would get close and then they would be rejected by the game. They could see the different levels of the game, but they couldn't set up an account as a player or see what other players were doing. The group seemed to be on the cutting edge of discovery about the killer, and no one else wanted to look at any other facts or evidence given the importance of the online game. Jill didn't like standing around waiting for the answers to come from someone else.

She signaled to the non-geeks to get them to follow her to another room. Fortunately, Jo had another living room in the lower level of her house, and Jill led everyone there. She could tell the detectives followed her reluctantly; they wanted to stay near the geeks as it seemed they would have an answer before anyone else.

"We can't help the geeks upstairs as they seem to be speaking a foreign language. I assume the FBI sent its best and brightest computer expert, knowing the circumstances of this case. So how can the rest of us contribute to the case? Let's review where we are. Forensically, we know that our victims died alone in their homes and the weapon was a knife that caused lacerations of the heart. We have a suspected killer who drove a pick-up truck. All of the victims died on the same night and were placed in the abandoned house, boat, and van on that same night. I performed the strangest autopsies ever with these victims as they were encased in ice, but I think that was more a reflection of the weather than the killer. What else do we know?"

Detective Van Lanen added, "We know that the victims were day-shift workers who would be alone the night of the murders. We also know there is little connection among these victims as they didn't socialize in each other's circles. We also know that baseball trading cards were left at each scene as proof tokens for the killer. We also know that the victims were diabetics. We haven't heard from the FBI's profiler yet; perhaps you have enough to make a statement about our killer?"

Agent Hall, who had been introduced earlier when she entered the house, said, "I find this to be a very unusual case. Many murderers are dominant in their behavior—they have a reason to kill and do it under their own direction. They're independent operators. This killer is willing to follow the orders of an unknown gamemaster. What I don't know is, did he design how these people were killed or was he given instructions on how to carry out these murders?"

She paused to take a breath and think about what

she'd observed in the murder scene and in the various reports she'd read from the police. Then she continued with her analysis: "Most murderers kill to control or to erase. This one kills to *belong*. He needs approval from someone he's never met—someone promising points, levels, or purpose."

The room was silent except for the faint keyboard clicking upstairs. Jill glanced toward the ceiling, where the techs were chasing ghosts through code. "So he's not only a killer," she said, "he's a student—following directions from a teacher or leader he worships."

"Exactly," Agent Hall replied. "Your autopsy notes mention repetition—a single killing stab wound, always to the heart. There are additional stab wounds, but they seemed to occur as the killer was trying to find the heart. It wasn't done with rage; rather it was inexperience, likely with instructions from the gamemaster."

Nathan exhaled slowly. "A soldier following orders."

Agent Hall nodded. "Or a gamer following a quest."

Jo's expression tightened. "You're saying the game is in charge of him."

"In a sense," Jill said. "The game, the person running it—someone. He's following directions and he achieves new levels in the game."

A dull thump from upstairs drew their eyes to the stairwell. A moment later, Henrik leaned over the railing, phone in hand. "We may have cracked part of the firewall," he said. "Lea's running a trace—it looks like the server bounces through Eastern Europe."

Agent Hall's brow furrowed. "That could mean

we're dealing with an offshore gamemaster—an enemy of the United States manipulating our citizens for evil purposes."

"Or a clever local hiding behind offshore servers," Henrik added. "Give us another hour."

"Do it," the agent said, then looked back at Jill. "When the FBI's profiler team joins me, we'll build a more expansive behavioral model. For now, assume your killer is male, mid-thirties to forties, intelligent enough to mask his tracks, and physically capable of moving bodies. Likely employed in a trade that gives him privacy, tools, and trucks."

Jill scribbled notes. "Someone comfortable around houses, maybe who's been in this neighborhood before. Construction, pest control, deliveries."

Agent Hall smiled faintly. "Dr. Quint, you might just might written the first line of my report."

Henrik disappeared from the railing upstairs. Jill rose, stretching her shoulders. "Let's call it for now. I've been working on this case since early this morning and my brain needs a break," she said. "We all could use a brain break."

"We have dinner plans and then tickets to the light-show at the Botanical Garden."

They soon sorted everyone, and the detectives and agents left with Lea's contact information.

They drifted toward coats and coffee mugs. Marie collected empty cups; Jo began stacking her dish-washer. Daylight was coming to an end as they had just passed the shortest day of day of the year.

Nathan brushed Jill's sleeve. "You're already building your list of suspects, aren't you?"

"I am," she admitted. "One teacher, one student. Now we just have to figure out if the teacher and student still want to play this awful game."

"Later," he said gently. "We need to socialize with our friends."

Somewhere in the neighborhood, a dog barked once, twice, then fell silent. Jill paused, scanning the dark shapes of the houses—most occupied, a few missing their owners at this moment, one empty that had held five victims' remains. Was the killer even now in the neighborhood?

She slid into the car beside Nathan. The heater fan whispered to life, fogging the windshield. "Five people," she murmured. "And a killer who thinks it's a game."

Nathan reached for her hand. "Then we beat him at it, but first dinner and lights."

The wipers cleared the windshield, revealing the road ahead gleaming with ice and headlights, a thin ribbon of light threading through the darkness. As they drove toward the restaurant, the faint blue glow from Jo's house—Henrik's computers still working upstairs, likely at the direction of his niece—followed them like an unblinking eye.

They arrived at the restaurant and managed to keep the conversation on lighter topics like the restaurant's dishes and where Jill and Henrik were going with new grape varietals. It was a perfect evening of friendship and conversation at the restaurant, followed by a walk through the cold but colorful holiday lights at the Botanical Gardens. When they ended the night, Henrik went with Marie to her house, so Jill wasn't going to get any updates on the computer search from him or Lea that evening. She knew, though, that if they had any breakthroughs, they would tell her.

CHAPTER 12

The next morning Jill, Jo, Marie, Henrik, Matthew, and Angela gathered in Jo's kitchen to discuss the updates. Henrik's people had been busy overnight. They had found new footage of the suspect truck with the help of additional neighborhood doorbell cameras. The additional footage confirmed the make and model, but it also showed that a noticeable light on the driver-side front of the truck was burned out. That feature allowed it to be tracked with ease, and they went back to all the neighborhood cameras looking for the same burned-out light.

Jill was finally getting reports back on the evidence she had collected during the autopsy. Liquids on all of the victims' clothing proved that at one time they had been stacked together, probably in the truck bed. There were some additional and unknown DNA traces on some locations on their clothing. However, that DNA could belong to their children or someone they had hugged. It was not definitive to convict the killer. It also didn't serve to identify the killer as the lab had been unable to link the DNA to anyone on file.

Angela had a photoshoot scheduled for the next day and asked, "With the limited time I have left to help on this case, what else can I do?"

Jill thought for a moment about Angela's skills. She was an expert at getting stories out of people, and she generally had her camera ready to grab images of the world around them. Since she had managed to get nearly all of the neighbors to allow them access to their security cameras, that was a huge win for their group.

"Your work yesterday in gaining access to the neighborhood cameras has been a huge win for us—now we know to look for the truck with the missing headlight, and we have a make and model. That is some of the most concrete information we've gained so far with this case. I guess all you can do today is help us brainstorm. Sorry I don't have anything more concrete than that for you."

"That's the conclusion I reached as well, so you're just verifying my thoughts. What I might do is take a picture of the truck and ask some more neighbors if they've seen it."

"That's an excellent idea! I should have thought of that. Jo, do you have a printer so Angela can print some copies of the best picture we have of the truck?"

"Just send it to Matthew and he'll get it printed." For

all of Jo's magic with numbers, she was a technophobe at home.

The group went to work finding the best picture of the truck, then Matthew and Angela went to another room to make copies. Henrik felt his phone vibrate and picked it up to read. Everyone was silent, hoping for a miracle identification of the killer or gamemaster.

"My staff sent me a report reflecting the times the truck visited the neighborhood going back several months where possible. It was here mostly during daytime hours during the summer, so perhaps he has an occupation that is generally tied to the daytime like landscaping, painting, or some task like that."

"That's excellent information, Henrik. I doubt our suspect works on landscaping as we don't have any pictures of a trailer being hauled behind the truck."

"That's true," Marie said. "So that leaves construction and the building trades, pest control, or just a worker on a crew that builds or remodels. Jo, are you aware of any ongoing construction projects in your neighborhood?"

"Yes. One of the neighbors bought a house last winter and has been remodeling it, but I think they've been finished for the past month. I guess he could have been working on that, but given his entry into the neighborhood, he was taking a roundabout way to get to the house he was working at."

"So maybe we're back to someone else in the neighborhood. Let's brainstorm. We already suggested painting and pest control. What other companies come to the neighborhood regularly or service more than one home?" Marie said.

"Tree-trimming workers. Yes, someone drives big trucks full of equipment or a wood chipper, but some of the workers show up in their own vehicles," Jo commented.

"Security firms?" Henrik suggested.

Jo shook her head and said, "If anyone is worried about security here, then they have a doorbell camera."

"Food delivery? Package delivery is almost always in an identifiable van and not a pick-up truck," Nathan said.

Jill nodded and added that to her list.

"Just small renovations where someone is here for a week or two by themselves or with one additional worker. I've had solar panels, a generator, and a sprinkler system installed, but those were all one- or two-day tasks, so yes, there may have been workers who assisted in their own vehicles, but they're one and done," Jo suggested.

"How about carpet cleaning? Again, though, they arrive in a van, not a truck. I would add car detailing, but this doesn't seem like a neighborhood that would be popular in," Angela said. "How about charity vans for seniors? Then again, that's never a truck."

"There's always the postman, but they would drive a mail truck. The cable company was here a lot last summer when cable first arrived in my neighborhood, but they haven't been around recently, and they have the company name on the side of the truck.

"I've seen some of those grass-fertilizer companies with a tank and a big hose in the back of the truck, or how about the utility company? Except, like Jo said, their name is on the side of the truck, and we've seen no name on our mysterious truck no matter how many different doorbell cam pictures we have," Marie stated. Her first suggestion was added to the list.

"I would add vehicle glass replacement, but that's also a one-and-done service in the neighborhood," Matthew suggested. "The same with window washing and gutter cleaning."

Jill waited for any other suggestions, but no one could think of anything to add. "So I think we've narrowed it to food delivery, pest control, tree trimming, or spraying lawns with fertilizer. Did I miss anything?"

She looked around and received nods that they were finished with their list.

"When I take the picture of the truck around the neighborhood, I'll ask if the residents use pest control, food delivery, tree trimming, or lawn spraying," Angela said, picking up copies of the truck photo that Matthew had printed.

"That's an excellent idea, Angela. Do you have pen and paper to take with you?" Jo asked. With a negative shake of Angela's head, Jo went upstairs to find those items in her kitchen junk drawer.

"Henrik, could your crew hack into the Wisconsin DMV to search for the make and model and then do a cross-search for the four types of businesses that might regularly visit this neighborhood? At least Wisconsin has a smaller population compared to California, so we should get a lot fewer hits," Jill said.

"Unless the truck is registered in Michigan, which is an hour away," Marie said.

"Darn, I forgot about the other state being so close. Maybe we'll luck out with Wisconsin."

"You're asking me as a visitor to your country to use my company resources to hack into a state-owned database?" Henrik asked.

"Yes. I suppose I could call the detective and Agent Hall and let them know where we're going with the investigation, but they have been silent and I consider that it's a two-way street when working on a case and sharing updates."

"Don't make them too mad or they won't buy my system," Henrik said with a smirk.

"As your imaginary VP of company sales, I think they will overlook the behavior of their civilian consultant as your system has the power to help them solve crimes. Besides, what's one more law enforcement agency? Don't you have enough clients?" Jill fired back.

"It's world domination. I want every law enforcement agency to use my software."

Marie clapped Henrik on the shoulder and said, "That sounds like too much work. I thought you were going to try and relax a little."

"Well, yes, once your friend agrees to come to work for me. She's really good at selling my technology."

"Not going to happen, Buddy," Nathan said. "How

will she manage her vineyard from Germany? You don't give up trying to hire her, do you?"

Henrik laughed and said, "No. Okay, back to work. Let me see if I can hack into your government database."

An idea came to Nathan, and he asked. "Have you tried to trace the baseball trading cards yet?"

There were a few seconds of silence before Jill said, "No, but that's a great idea, Honey. Anyone know how we can do that? I don't even know where they're sold."

"I've collected a few cards," Matthew admitted. "Let me look into that. I know you can buy packs from all major retailers—online and in-store. There are also memorabilia and collector shops in town. I think we should first find the value of the cards left at the murder scene as that will likely determine the source."

"That's a great idea. Thanks, Matthew. I know you're somewhat new to these investigations and this is the first in your neighborhood, but thanks for thinking of a way to pursue Nathan's suggestion."

He nodded and said, "Anything to keep Jo safe. I'm going to grab my laptop and start searching."

"I wonder if it is the killer or the gamemaster who likes baseball cards as proof tokens?" Marie said.

"That's another good question, Marie," Jill said. "Henrik, would Lea be able to determine that? I know your staff got into the video game, but I don't know how far they were able to go through the game."

"I will ask about the vehicle search, the proof tokens,

and if they can do a separate search for baseball cards, even though Matthew is also working on that," he said.

"Okay, what else can we work on? Angela has her assignment, as does Henrik," Marie asked.

Matthew looked up from the laptop he was using to search for the playing cards and said, "None of the baseball cards found at the victims' houses are valuable even if they were in good condition. I just tried to buy these five specifically and they're in a special pack of cards sold together. They're sold directly by the Topps Company, which used to sell all baseball trading cards until the company was bought out in 2022. I could find the set at some online commerce stores, and I thought I would try calling the stores in town that might carry this pack. Your suspect could easily have bought the cards individually, but the pack seems the easiest way to get them."

"How many cards are in this pack?" Jill asked, wondering if their suspect would be killing more people.

"132."

"That's bad news. Will we have another 127 deaths as a result of the killer or the gamemaster? I sure hope not. Why don't you look up the addresses of stores in Green Bay that sell baseball cards, or maybe you and Angela could interview the store owners once she's done with her neighborhood canvass."

Matthew nodded and said he would wait for Angela's return.

"For once, this seems to be a case where you don't need my financial wizardry," Jo said.

"Yes, I can't think of when that last happened with a case. Maybe at some point Henrik will have enough information about our gamemaster to make him worthy of financial scrutiny. Creating and operating an online video game in the dark recesses of the internet takes coding skills. I can't imagine our gamemaster paying someone skilled who does computer coding to create this monstrous game."

CHAPTER 13

*J*ill knew there was nothing she could
personally do at the moment to help solve
the case. Their killer had covered his tracks
as well as in any case she'd been a part of. Still, it could
be worse, she had to remind herself. They could have
dumped the bodies in the frozen wilderness of Wisconsin, where they might not be discovered for years or
their remains might be subject to animal attacks.

She sighed and wished she could make Henrik's
team work faster. She knew she shouldn't complain—
she was lucky to have such technical resources as she
didn't understand enough about computers to accelerate solving these cases. Certainly, even if she understood computers better, she could never match Lea's
hacking talents.

Maybe she should give the detective a call to see if
he had learned anything through the search of the

DMV database with the new photos of the vehicle that she had sent him. She grabbed her phone off the kitchen island and punched in the number for the detective.

"Yes, Dr. Quint?"

"Hello, Detective. I wondered if you would share with me what you found in the DMV database regarding our suspect vehicle?"

There was a pause at the other end of the phone as he probably thought about the illegality of sharing private information with her. On the other hand, the department was under pressure to solve the five murders. No one in town felt safe at the moment. So she added, "You might guess that I have the computer resources to eventually find that information myself, but it's faster if you already have it."

She heard him sigh and he replied, "I'm sharing this with you because we may need forensic evidence from the vehicle once we find it."

"That works for me," Jill said, knowing that she wouldn't be called to examine a vehicle as that was the duty of crime scene investigators. She was grateful for any cooperation she received from Detective Van Lanen.

"I just sent the list to your email address. Tell me you won't be calling any of these people and asking about their vehicle."

"I can confirm that, Detective. I'll call you with any conclusions I make about the vehicle."

"Thank you and keep me informed," he said before ending the call.

Jill did a little happy dance before looking at the email the detective sent.

Nathan smiled at her and said, "In a rare occurrence for Dr. Jill Quint, local law enforcement is cooperating and sharing some information with her."

"Yep, I just opened the email with a list of vehicles that might match our suspect vehicle. Let's go to work looking at it. Henrik, let Lea know we got it through legitimate means."

Jill opened up her laptop and opened the file. Wisconsin had 1.1 million pick-up trucks registered. Green Bay was the third largest city so that brought her total down to less than a third. The police requested a list of registrations within thirty miles of Green Bay and that had narrowed her list fewer than twenty thousand trucks. Once it was narrowed further by color, make, and model, she was down to about forty trucks.

"So I have forty truck owners to research. Marie, Jo, Nathan, how about if the four of us take ten truck owners each and see what we can find out about them? Specifically we're looking for someone involved in one of the four targeted businesses."

"It's been a while since I've helped on one of your cases. I usually just cook meals and provide wine," Nathan said. "Refresh me on what websites I use to investigate my ten."

As Marie was the expert at finding background information, she briefed all of them about where to look for information. Soon there was quiet in the room as everyone searched the internet and made notes about what they found. A little more than an hour later, their research had narrowed it to three men, but really, one man rose to the top of Jill's list.

His name was Logan Web, and he operated a small pest control company. He was 6'2" tall and 220 pounds. He was big enough to move the victims' remains. Strangely enough, he had been a minor league ball player nearly a decade ago. Single, with no children and not especially active on social media.

She asked Henrik to determine if he played the Murder-Rage video game. She wished she could have sent Angela and Matthew out with his picture, but that would be stepping way over the line. She was running on instinct and research, but she had no evidence. Instead, she called the detective.

"Yes, Dr. Quint?" seemed to be Detective Van Lanen's go-to terse phone answer. At least he wasn't ignoring her.

"So, my team reviewed all the truck owners on your list. One of those owners is Logan Web, and I think you should perhaps pull him in for an interview or at least take a look at his truck to see if it's missing a light on the driver's side front."

"Why?"

"We sent you the photos of the suspect truck and you know it's missing a light. He also operates a pest control company which gives him a reason to scout the neighborhood. He's big enough to move bodies and he's a former minor league baseball player. We're trying to find out if he's a player in the Murder-Rage game."

"He's on our list as well, but we haven't limited it to a single suspect as there is no evidence at the present linking him to these murders. Do you have any other new information for me?"

"No, that's it, Detective. Could someone go by the man's house at least and see if he has a burned-out light on the truck?"

"You realize that's weak evidence."

"Of course, but I always start with weak evidence and build on it. Like, if the light is not working on the truck, maybe you could subpoena his phone records to see if he was near the victims' houses on the night of the murder. Again, that's not enough to convict him with, but at least your department could keep an eye on him. Do you know that the five baseball trading cards that were left at the scene come in a pack of 132 cards? I don't know if he plans more murders to level up, but one would hope he's not planning on all 132," Jill said.

"I'll run that by my FBI colleagues. They're the experts on behavior," was the detective's only response before ending the call.

"Did you get anywhere with the detective?" Marie asked.

"I don't think so. Logan Web is one of many on their list. He seemed to think I narrowed the list of suspects too quickly," Jill mused.

"In my vast experience with you on a murder case, your gut instinct is rarely if ever wrong," Nathan said.

"Thank you, Sweetie. Let's switch names on the truck list and research them again to see if anyone else pops up."

"Or we could find his home address and go check out the lights on the truck," Marie suggested.

"The trouble with that is we don't know if the light is missing or the bulb is burned out. If the bulb is burned out, we would need to see the truck in the dark with the vehicle turned on. Also, in the back of my head I keep thinking he might have fixed the light by now."

"That's all true. Plus if he parks the truck at his business, then going to his home doesn't do any good. Okay, let's swap names and go back over our forty or so truck owners."

After fresh eyes looked at each name, Logan Web remained their prime suspect. Angela returned and Jill updated her on their progress. "Neighbors thought they might have seen the truck but were unsure" was Angela's summary of the neighbors' comments. Vehicles came and went all the time for a variety of reasons, and there was no reason for one truck to stand out.

Matthew and Angela were going to leave to interview the shop owners who sold collectible baseball cards. They had the home address of their suspect and would drive by his residence in between stores on the off chance they would see something of interest.

"We seem to be back to needing new information from Henrik's crew. I can't think of anything else to do for this case at the moment," Jill said, disappointment in her voice.

"I'll do a deep dive on Logan Web to see if I come up with anything new," Marie said.

"I'll look him up on all the databases I know of for financial, tax, and legal proceedings," Jo added.

"I'll cook lunch," Nathan said.

"You're all the best," Jill declared, giving each a hug.

With her friends hard at work searching for new information and Nathan taking care of their empty stomachs, Jill went back to the autopsies to see if there were any clues she had missed. She was given access to the five records only, but some of the crime scene information was shared, so that was new information as it was analyzed and results were reported.

There were reports about the order of the placement of the victims' remains in the truck and, therefore, the route the killer took. Another piece of interesting information was the baseball trading cards. The backside of each card featured a micro-dot QR code, an addition that was not typically included on the cards. The micro-dot code was much smaller than the traditional-sized code. The QR codes took the techs to a spreadsheet where a player completed a form about leveling up. Jill wondered who added the QR code—the player or the gamemaster.

Nathan called them together for lunch, setting aside plates for Matthew and Angela once they returned from talking to the stores that sold cards.

CHAPTER 14

When Henrik for lunch, he gave them an update of the work his company was doing to break into the Murder-Rage game. "We've managed to enter the game. We have a list of all the players and specifically the one who uploaded the base-ball cards from your murder scene. We haven't figured out who the gamemaster is other than he goes by the name Shezmu. For those of you who have never heard of that name, he was an Egyptian god of blood, and he could slaughter other deities. I don't think this means that our gamemaster is from Egypt rather, I'm explaining the suitability of his name to the game."

"The more we delve into this game, the more I loathe every aspect of it," Jill said. "Do you have any idea how long the game has been going on or how many real-life deaths it has caused?"

"No, our focus is on connecting the player to your

murders and finding the real person behind the gamemaster. We wasted time trying to hack into your license bureau, but fortunately you found another source for that information."

"Yes we did, and we have a number one suspect. Marie is doing a deep dive into his background, and Jo into his finances, but maybe you can connect his real name with his player name. His real name is Logan Web and he provides pest control for Jo's neighborhood," Jill said. "Also, I read the crime scene information, and these baseball cards each had a micro-dot QR code that is an aftermarket add-on that takes you to an online form to complete to use for leveling up. You wouldn't immediately know it was used for Murder-Rage."

Henrik pulled out his cellphone and sent their suspect's name with instructions to his team, then he said, "We never starve when Nathan is in the kitchen. It looks like we have a taco bar laid out for our eating pleasure."

"That's correct, and I'm sure much to Jill's delight, I've paired the taco bar with Sangria."

"I love Sangria, and perhaps the fruit at the bottom is one of my daily servings of fruits and vegetables," Jill said, drinking the sweet wine concoction. "What else besides beer would you serve with tacos?"

Everyone smiled, knowing that Nathan had made them a perfect lunch and Jill was satisfied with her sweet Sangria. It was a nice break from the depressing scenario of the video game and its intent of killing people to level up.

Henrik's phone beeped and conversation stopped as he pulled his phone from his pocket. "You know, guys, this could be a message regarding my business. There's no need to pause your conversation for me."

"It could be, but somehow I would think you do most business communication through email where you have a paper trail. Any news for us?" Jill asked just as Matthew and Angela walked into the kitchen.

"Yes, we have Logan Web's player name. It's 'BadSpider5.'"

"That fits with his pest control job," Angela remarked.

"What did you guys find? Anything?" Jill asked. She was about to call the detective again and she may as well deliver all the news at once.

"We have a shop owner who vaguely remembered your suspect, and we went by his house, but didn't see the truck."

"I would guess there is a much-reduced workload for pest control in the winter as the little beasties should all be frozen," Marie said. "I need to dive deeper into his background to see what he does in the winter to occupy himself."

"I know the answer to that," Jo said. "He does snow removal. I saw that his business license stated he did pest control and snow removal. Other than a bankruptcy perhaps five years ago, I didn't see any court action against him. Not even a speeding ticket."

"Wow, speeding tickets are almost a rite of passage," Jill said, having been pulled over by law enforcement for several speeding violations in her lifetime.

"You have many speeding violations? Perhaps you wouldn't pass the background check to come to work for me," Henrik said.

"It's a good thing I'm not coming to work for you, then," Jill quipped. "I'm going to call the detective with our new information," she said, stepping out of the kitchen and into Jo's living room.

She dialed the detective's number, but he didn't answer, so she left a voicemail with their latest findings and returned to the kitchen.

Nathan had heated the food for Angela and Matthew and they were in the midst of eating. It wasn't a good time to bring up murder. They talked about the various stores and what they sold, and then they went completely off-topic and talked about the upcoming Green Bay Packers game against the Minnesota Vikings, who were usually fierce competitors but had been struggling this season with injuries in their young quarterback.

Jill's cellphone rang and she saw from the caller ID that it was the detective. "Hello, Detective. Did you get my message?"

"Yes, I'm calling to notify you that the FBI is sending over their computer expert, Agent Stevenson, to understand how you found Logan Web's name on the video game. We are also bringing him in for questioning."

"That's awesome. Do you have enough evidence to

put a tracer on his cellphone to understand his movements on the night of the murder?"

"You know, Dr. Quint, you and your team have been helpful with this case, but you're also a pain in the ass. I follow one of your clues and you ask me to follow another five."

"Sorry, Detective, that's just the way I work. I really want the case solved before he levels up through additional murders. Do you know if the FBI has gotten anywhere with identifying the gamemaster?"

"I called to invite you to listen to our interview with Logan, not answer another five questions. Are you interested? My office would call you when he's on his way to the station."

"Yes, I would be interested in that. Thanks, Detective."

"Okay, well, my office will call when we have a time for the interview."

Just before he was going to end the call, she added, "My people went by his house, but the suspect truck was not visible."

Jill smiled when she heard a sigh at the other end of the phone and then he ended the call.

She returned to the kitchen with a smile on her face. "The police are going to bring Logan in for questioning and they've invited me to listen. Also, the FBI geek is on his way to speak with you, Henrik," Jill finished just as Jo's doorbell rang.

"What put a smile on your face?" Marie asked.

"The detective told me that I was a pain in his ass as

he would call with the answer to one question and then he would be subject to five questions from me. That's quite a compliment considering he still invited me to listen to their interview. I even got a second sigh out of him when I told him that Angela and Matthew went by Web's house and the truck wasn't there, or at least visible. I'm amused that I annoy him yet he's keeping me around because we're helping solve the case."

Jo went to her front door, finding the referenced FBI person standing on her stoop. She invited him in and took him over to Henrik. He wanted a demo from Henrik as likely one day he would be called to testify in court about evidence. Henrik would much rather teach an American law enforcement representative about how he found evidence so that the officer can demonstrate to a court, rather than get called to testify himself.

Since the detective hadn't answered all her questions, she decided to ask the FBI agent. "Has your agency or the police department gotten a subpoena to triangulate Logan Web's movements?"

The agent looked like a deer caught in the headlights. He knew he shouldn't answer any civilian questions, but with this question in particular, he thought the good doctor's friend who was teaching him new computer skills could likely do it unofficially.

"Yes, Dr. Quint, the detective was walking through a subpoena for the phone tracking. They need it to see if they can track his movements and potentially to find him now for questioning."

"Thank you, Agent Stevenson."

Jill was satisfied that everything was being done that could be done with regard to the case. If the police got the phone records and interviewed Logan Web today, they might be able to arrest him today. Of course, that wouldn't get rid of the video game or arrest the gamemaster behind this horrible game, but in theory Logan's arrest would make Jo's neighborhood and city safer.

A few hours went by, and still no call from the detective, so Jill called him. "Have you found Logan Web?"

"I was just about to call you. We finally located him and we'll be interviewing him within the next thirty minutes. Will you be coming?"

"Yes. See you soon," Jill said, ending the call.

"The police have Logan Web in custody and I'm heading over to the station to observe the interview. Be back soon."

"Ah, Jill, do you know where the police department is?" Jo asked.

"No, I figured I would just put it in my GPS."

"It's very close to city hall—if you're near a gold domed building with a statue of the French explorer Jean Nicolet out front, then you're almost there."

"Thanks, Jo." Jill said, putting on her coat and gathering a notebook to take with her.

As she was walking out the door, she heard Nathan say, "She always manages to have murder business when it's time to do the dishes." She stuck her head back in and beamed a smile at him before leaving.

Jill entered the address into her GPS and drove toward the police department. When she arrived and checked in at the front desk, she was given a temporary badge, and a volunteer walked her to where the detective was. Another detective took Jill to a room where she could observe the conversation between two detectives and Logan Web.

"If I want to get a message to the detective, can I text him?" Jill asked.

"Probably. Every detective works differently during interviews; some can multitask and look at texts from their helpful co-workers outside the interview room, others lose concentration and flow and won't do it. Detective Van Lanen has been a text reader in the past, but I can't guarantee that this interview will work that way."

Jill nodded and looked at their suspect through the one-way glass. He was as his driver's license described—late 20s, brown hair, strong-looking 6'2" frame. He looked fit and capable of the fireman's carry of the victims. She hadn't heard the detective read Logan his rights, but that easily could have happened before she arrived. The detective was writing down the basics— age, full name, address, and occupation. Good, she hadn't missed much of the interview.

"Mr. Web, can you tell us where you were on the night of December 21 of this year?" the detective asked.

Logan had the briefest of hesitation before he

responded without emotion, "Asleep in my bed as I usually am after about eleven at night. I work during the day and sleep at night."

"Can anyone verify that?"

"No. I live alone."

"Do you hunt Mr. Web? Deer? Bear?"

"Yes, doesn't everyone in this state?"

"Thank you."

The detective next asked him about the make and model of the truck that was spotted by the door cameras both before and during the night of the murders. Logan indicated that that was his work truck.

"Where do you keep your truck? We didn't notice it in your driveway when we looked for you earlier."

"At the end of the pest control season each year, I have the truck serviced, so it's at the mechanic's shop."

The detective asked for the location of the suspect's vehicle. The light defect might be repaired by now, but they could scan the truck's bed with luminol and then swab any spots to see if the fluids belonged to any of the five victims. Even if he had taken it through the car wash, it was likely that there would be trace evidence.

"Thank you, Mr. Web. One moment please," Detective Van Lanen said as he texted something into his phone. Jill presumed he was sending the CSI team over to check out the truck.

The detective continued to ask him questions, but he knew that while he agreed with Dr. Quint that Logan Web was their suspect, he unfortunately didn't have enough to hold him. That might change in a few hours when the CSI team had had a chance to review the truck. If the luminol was positive, then Logan might say that it was from a dead deer, and they would have to wait on lab testing for confirmation of human versus animal blood. At this point, he didn't even have enough to obtain a search warrant for his house to look for the murder weapon—the knife—or the baseball trading cards. Finding the pack of cards with the five cards from the murder scenes missing would be quite a damning piece of evidence.

Eventually, the interview came to an end and the detective escorted Mr. Web to where an officer would return him to his home. Once he was gone, the detective returned to where Jill was and asked," So, what do you think?"

"Sadly, at the moment, you don't have enough evidence to hold him or probably even to get a search warrant for his house. We can only hope that the truck tests positive for luminol and that the blood proves to be human rather than from, say, a deer as Web might say he hunted."

"That was my conclusion. Still, I was able to get a court-approved subpoena to track his phone's GPS, so as soon as the telephone company hands over the records, we might see some evidence therein."

"Unless he used a burner phone for the night of the murders," Jill suggested.

"Except he had a digital watch on, and depending on the phone and the watch that may leave a trail."

"Yes, maybe you'll be lucky. Kudos to you for

noticing the watch; that escaped my notice. I will say he looked sufficiently strong to move the bodies."

"Yes, I noticed that too. What's the FBI expert doing?"

"That's above my pay grade. He's speaking geek to Henrik and his employees. I'm sure he'll report to you once he has news."

"Were you tempted to send any questions to me via text during the interview?" the detective surprisingly asked.

"No. I knew you had constraints around what you could ask, and I also knew that Logan Web could have walked out of that interview at any time. So I think you got as much out of him as was possible. If you have nothing more, I'll head home and see what my gang is up to—we had a few more clues we were looking at."

The detective nodded and said, "Keep me informed."

Jill concurred and went back the way she came in, dropping off her temporary badge at reception before she left.

CHAPTER 15

Jill drove home thinking about the next steps. She felt like they were closing in on Logan Web. Either the CSI team would come through, or Henrik's team would. When she arrived home, she was greeted with news from her friends that Henrik's team had had a breakthrough.

"We've broken into the game and specifically linked BadSpider5 with Logan Web. My FBI colleague is working with the police to get a search warrant for Logan's house. Once we got into his account, we also saw pictures of the tools he needed to commit his crimes in a storage unit. So they're also getting a search warrant for his financial records to find the rent payment and therefore the storage unit's location. I've taught the FBI agent how to break into the game and gather evidence for his future testimony."

"Wow, all in the hour I was gone. It seems like your work is done here."

"It seems sudden, but my best staff have been trying to break into the video game for days. I'm just glad they were able to do it and uphold my sterling reputation with all of you," he said with a smile.

"You'll always have a sterling reputation with me. You've helped with so many cases. Does that mean you're about to leave Marie and the rest of us to jet off to parts unknown?"

"Yes, unfortunately. Marie is going to cook dinner for me this evening and then I'm heading back to Germany. I have grapes to bottle, you know."

"In winter? Are you making ice wine?"

"Just testing your wine knowledge and you passed," Henrik said with a grin.

Jill gave him a slight arm slug and then a hug, and soon he and Marie departed for some alone time before they were again separated for a couple of months. Both had been married before and neither had the desire to marry a second time. Their long-distance relationship worked for them.

Goodbyes were said and Jill returned to the case. Agent Stephenson was waiting to talk with Jill before departing as well.

"Dr. Quint, I must say that this is perhaps the most interesting case I've ever worked on, and I'm grateful for all that Mr. Klein and his staff taught me. I was familiar with his software as the FBI is a client, but his ability to reach the criminal corners of the internet is impressive. I'm going to recommend to the FBI leadership that they send a team to Germany to meet with his people and learn from them. They're probably stepping over the legal line per US privacy laws, but I definitely think we would catch criminals faster and we could go after the more heinous internet content like sex trafficking or child pornography. We'll find a balance in the agency."

"That's good news. Henrik is really a great guy who has helped us solve numerous crimes across multiple countries. I'm sure you'll be able to work something out between your agency and his company."

They shared a bit more conversation, and then the agent left Jo's house. Jo, Matthew, Nathan, Angela, and Jill looked at each other, trying to remember where they were in regard to investigating the case.

"I think our work is done for the most part. With the FBI having evidence of Logan Web's ties to the Murder-Rage video game, the police have sufficient evidence to detain him. They should be able to get subpoenas to search his phone records to track his movements, and search his house for the murder weapon or for the pack of the baseball trading cards," Jill said.

"That's good news. I have to go back to work tomorrow and I really wanted the suspect in custody because we gathered enough evidence to convict him," Angela said.

"Jill, I know that you and Nathan delayed your return to California so you could make my neighborhood safer, and I'd like to thank you for that. We'll just have our final dinner tonight assuming that you'll be flying home tomorrow?" Jo said.

"We haven't changed our reservation as the case came together a lot today, but yes, I'll look at confirming our booking for our flight tomorrow," Nathan said, pulling out his phone.

"The case isn't at an end and won't be for several years by the time it makes its way through the justice system, but Logan Web will be in custody and off the streets. I assume the FBI will work on finding the gamemaster and will work on ending the game and arresting him," Jill said. "So yes, we're good to go home. Someday I may have to fly back for testimony, but then again, they might allow me to videoconference into the courtroom to talk about the autopsy results. Who knows?"

Jill watched her phone for the remainder of the afternoon and evening, hoping for an update from the detective about the vehicle and the arrest of Logan Web, but all was quiet. She and her friends began a couple games of cards to while away their last night in Green Bay. She used her passcode to log into the autopsy results to see if the CSIs posted anything there, and she saw a match and smiled.

"Good news?" Nathan asked.

"Yes, they used luminol on our suspect's truck and it was positive for blood. Now there's a test result that includes DNA of one of the victims. I didn't open all of the records to see if they found matches to all of them, but the very fact that there is blood residue in the truck that matches one of the victims pretty well nails the coffin shut on Logan Web. I hope they have him in custody. In fact, I think I'll text the detective to make sure."

Jill sent off a message and then went back to the fierce card game they were playing. She had won the first round, but Jo was beating her this time.

A text arrived from the detective that said, in a nutshell, that they had issued an Attempt to Locate bulletin to lead to the arrest of Logan Web. The police were unable to find him. His truck was still at the mechanic's garage, but he was not answering his cell phone, nor had anyone seen him. Agent Stephenson had been able to log into the Murder-Rage game to find mention by the gamemaster that Logan had graduated from Silent Stalker to Master of Knives. He didn't find any posts by BadSpider5 in the last twelve hours or so.

Jill responded by asking about the phone tracker and if they had found the storage unit. The detective said they had, and he and the crime scene crew were heading toward it. Jill was welcome to join them at a specific address. They were close to the end of the card game, so the ever-curious Jill drove herself to the site of the storage unit as soon as the last card was played. Yep, she lost this round.

A short time later she arrived at a well-lit storage unit facility and parked behind another three cars to join Detective Van Lanen.

"What have you found in here?" she asked the glove-wearing detectives and crime scene staff.

"Plenty more evidence. It seems to indicate that Logan Web plans to kill more people in an attempt to level up in the video game. He has gloves, a tarp that I presume he uses to wrap the bodies, and most damning of all, records of his pest control clients, and our five victims all used his service."

"I don't think any of our victims envisioned that they were the pests that he planned to exterminate," Detective Hagstrom said.

"Sad and snarky, but true," Jill said.

A crime scene team member brought over a digital camera that had photos of the victims. It was creepy. Jill could see they had hit the motherlode of evidence in this storage unit. She looked around and couldn't think of anything she could add as either a PI or a forensic pathologist; as the law enforcement officers had the evidence collection well in hand.

"Detective, were you able to triangulate his phone?"

"Yes and no. Yes, a judge approved our accessing his cellular phone GPS pings, but the phone company hasn't delivered yet."

"Does Logan Web have another car besides the pick-up truck?"

"Yes. It is a part of our bulletin. Our FBI behavioral health expert is worried he might harm himself. 'People who follow charismatic leaders and don't get the love and attention they seek from such a leader are prone to harming themselves' was their comment. There are many isolated areas to hide. For his sake, I hope he's hiding rather than has harmed himself."

"Like so many of my cases, this is just so sad. Five lives were lost and a sixth one is hanging in the balance. We're not close to identifying the gamemaster who caused all of this. My German friend is on his way back home, but his team is still working on identifying the mastermind behind these terrible murders. I'm also curious and anxious to know whether any other murders were committed worldwide as a part of this game?"

Just then one of the CSIs called out, "Detective, we have a laptop. It was hidden under a few things. We just tried to turn it on, but it requires a password."

"Try BadSpider5 with the *B* and *S* capitalized," Jill suggested.

The tech did as Jill suggested and smiled. "We're in."

"I would suggest you call FBI Agent Stephenson; my friend taught him how to reach Murder-Rage, which is the video game that Logan Web was playing."

"That's a good suggestion. We don't have the computer expertise that he has, and maybe we can find more or new information about the game," the detective said, calling the agent.

"I'm going to head out. It looks like you have a long evening ahead of you cataloging this stuff, and I don't see anything I can add as a forensic pathologist. Also, Detective, I'm flying home tomorrow, so this is likely the last time you'll be seeing me. Of course, I'm quite reachable by phone if you should have any questions."

"On behalf of the citizens of Green Bay, I would like to thank you for your help with this case. Who knows if he would have leveled up in the game with more murders? We might never have solved it without your computer whiz. You are that rare civilian who has been helpful," Detective Van Lanen said, holding out his hand to shake hers before he pulled it back quickly, took off his latex glove, and then reached out again to shake.

Little did he know that he was wrong.

At around seven the next morning, she received a call from the detective.

"Sorry to call you so early, but we found Logan Web early this morning. Unfortunately, he is deceased. Our Medical Examiner is still on vacation. Would you have time to complete the autopsy before you catch your plane?"

"I'm a morning person, Detective, so this isn't early for me. Our flight leaves in the late afternoon, so I do indeed have time to help you out. I'll be there in about thirty minutes, if you'll clear the way for me at the ME's office."

Jill wondered how they found him, and was it self-inflicted. She didn't ask the detective as she liked to draw her own conclusions. She left a note for Jo and Nathan and took off for the Medical Examiner's office.

She went through the check-in process and soon was suited up and approached the autopsy table. The mortuary techs had taken routine x-rays and weighed Logan Web. She pulled up the data on that and lab work they had drawn and sent out for processing. She had access to where he was discovered, which was in a car. According to the report, they found him as he had turned his cell phone back on according to the telecom company. It looked like a gunshot to the head, but there was something off about the picture. Then it came to her—she remembered watching Logan Web during the interview and he was left-handed. The scene picture showed a gun in the right hand.

Before she started on the autopsy, she made a call to the detective. After he answered she asked. "Do you think Logan Web is a homicide or suicide?"

"You've barely had time to start an autopsy—what would make you think it was either designation?"

"You said yourself the FBI experts said he was prone to self-harm. However, your scene pictures show the gun in his right hand, and I know he was left-handed."

"Bingo, Dr. Quint, and kudos to you for picking up on that. I think it might be a homicide, though if it was, I wonder why his phone was turned on about an hour before we found him."

"I'll have to do some calculations to reach an approximate time of death once I look at his temperature, his clothing, and the outside temperature. Was his car running at the time you found him?"

"No. The engine was off but not completely cool yet. Let me know what you find, and thank you for your availability. Our ME is due back in three days and then we'll probably not have any suspicious death cases for months."

"Will do, Detective."

She ended the call and began performing calculations regarding the time of death. With the outside cold temperatures, she could narrow it to a few hours' range, but that was the best she could do. She texted the estimated time of death window as an FYI to the detective.

Sometime later, after she finished the autopsy, Jill was pulling off her gloves to do some computer work on her findings. Autopsy rooms were set up so that the pathologist could dictate as they performed their examination, but Jill liked to correct dictation errors and add information based on lab results. She posted additional lab work including eye potassium levels, but that didn't change her window on the time of death. A weird finding was that Mr. Web likely was also a diabetic. She didn't have access to his medical records, but the coincidence of both killer and victims all being diabetics was odd. They now knew that the connection between the victims and the killers was his pest control service, but a second and likely unrelated connection was diabetes.

She paused to text Marie, giving her a status on the case and asking if she remembered from any of her social media searches whether Logan had mentioned diabetes. Marie said she did not but would take a second look. It didn't change anything in the case, but maybe Logan as a former athlete was frustrated with the diabetes diagnosis when he was trying to be an athlete in top shape. Maybe it was a point of conversation with these particular pest control customers, though Jill would have thought that it would have made them harder to kill if he had established an empathetic connection with them. Anyone who could kill five people by stabbing them in the heart had serious mental issues, but as it was not her area of expertise, she would stop speculating on the topic.

She wrapped up her examination and corresponding paperwork and then entered the locker room to change back into her street clothes. Her conclusion at the end of the autopsy was that the manner of death was homicide due to a bullet injury to the brain. Someone tried to make it look like a suicide, but they had put the gun in the wrong hand and there weren't any powder burns. Law enforcement now had a sixth homicide to run down. That said, most of the town would be comforted to know that the murderer of five members of their community was solved and the killer was now dead, too, but who killed Logan Web?

The gamemaster had incredible coding skills to create his monstrous game and then be able to hold off most of law enforcement that wanted a view inside the game. That said, they knew that Logan Web might be a weak link to the game. Maybe he told the gamemaster about his police interview. If that was the case, then the gamemaster had to be located likely in the United States in order to reach Logan as quickly as he had. Who turned his phone on—Logan or his killer?

CHAPTER 16

Jill arrived at Jo's house just in time for a big lunch. They were departing around 4:30 and had a connection at a different airport before arriving at their home airport, Fresno. From there they had less than an hour drive to reach their home. It was a long journey and their house sitter would be departing as soon as he heard they had landed in Fresno. Nathan's cat Arthur and Jill's dog Trixie would be happy to greet them despite being spoiled by their house sitter.

"We saw your note. I was trying to think of the last case we had together when you performed an autopsy just before flying somewhere, and I couldn't think of one. Green Bay is lucky to have such a versatile visitor in you."

"Jo, you know that Nathan, Henrik, and I would do anything to make your neighborhood safe. In fact, if your meth dealer isn't locked up in the near future, we should plan a vacation around collecting evidence to put him away permanently. I know he isn't a bother as you're a few blocks away, but I'm sure he steals to support his drug habit."

"I like that idea. Not only would our usual team work on the case, but we could also involve the neighbors, allowing everyone to contribute to making the justice system work in the neighborhood's favor. It might almost be like an unwritten Agatha Christie novel."

"We could do that in the near future. Pick a week that works for everyone and is not grape-harvesting season and we will become the *Nicolet Anti-Meth Club* with a goal to get the meth dealing out of your neighborhood," Jill suggested.

"We need Henrik here so we can find the drug transactions on the phone or through social media or however the dealers are arranging the sales. My neighbors would be onboard, so you'll have like twenty people trying to collect evidence on our meth dealer," Jo said.

"Why don't you arrange that for late Spring? That gives everyone time to get their schedule in order, and it's before grape-harvesting season come summertime. Maybe the cops will have enough to lock him up before we get to that meeting, and we can always cancel if it is not necessary. As resident social queen, you can arrange things with Matthews's help."

Jo nodded and wrote herself a note to schedule said

meeting, then she asked, "So what's the latest on the case?"

"Logan Web is dead; that's who I autopsied this morning as the local ME is still away on vacation. He was shot in the head, though his killer tried to make it look like suicide."

"That's not good that he was killed, right? I mean, beyond the obvious that it's never good when someone is dead, I would guess the number one suspect is the gamemaster."

"That's also my thought, and I'm going to warn Henrik that if the gamemaster can identify BadSpider5's real name and home address, then all the work Lea and the others did hacking into his website might be traceable also, and he might go after them. I know that his company is working on identifying who the gamemaster is, but we have a clue from Logan Web's death—he was murdered about seven to nine hours after the police interviewed him. I would think he went home and notified the gamemaster of the police interview," Jill said.

"That means that the gamemaster is likely physically living in the United States," Matthew said.

"Yes, that was one of my thoughts. Even if the gamemaster was rich. It still would have taken time to arrange a private jet to get here in time if they came from Europe or Asia or even South America," Jill said.

"How about the gamemaster going after you, Jill?" Nathan asked, always worried about his wife.

"I didn't get into his video game, and why would he go after your run-of-the-mill medical examiner? I think Henrik and his crew are more likely targets, or Agent Stephenson or Detective Van Lanen."

"That true, though I would never call you run of the mill," Nathan replied as he and Jo dished out food onto plates.

"Another thing I discovered during his autopsy is that he was also a diabetic as he had a high A1C. I wasn't able to review his medical records to know if the condition was diagnosed or if he didn't know he had the condition. It's kind of weird to me that besides being clients of his pest control company, all of his victims were also diabetics. You would have thought he would have empathy for his fellow diabetics."

"That is weird, and I agree with you that I would've thought he'd have had more empathy for his fellow diabetics," Jo said.

"Yes, I thought of that also, but remember he was a former athlete who tried to break into major league baseball. Perhaps his diabetes made that impossible and in some twisted way he was angry about any person with diabetes. Remember, he killed five people to level up in a video game. That's not quite the mind of a mentally sound individual."

"True that. So what are your and the police's next steps?"

"I would guess that they will announce that the murder of the five individuals is solved and the killer is dead. The public won't care who killed the killer. I'm guessing they'll hold a press conference later today in conjunction with the FBI and they'll talk about the Murder-Rage video game. Meanwhile, the police have a wealth of forensic information in Logan Web's storage shed including a laptop that they hope may have more information about the video game or gamemaster. The detectives now need to solve Logan Web's murder, but this case of the video game murders is so sensational, I fear they'll be distracted until the attention over the case dies down."

"Jill, do you have any more work to do on the case?" Matthew asked. This was the first case that he had watched Jo and her girlfriends try to solve. It was interesting pairing up with Angela to talk with the neighbors and baseball trading card shop owners. He had to admit, though, that it was a very strange situation.

"I'll check in on some test results that aren't back yet for Logan Web, but basically, there is nothing more I can do. Marie did a little more investigation of Logan to see if he mentioned diabetes, but that was a dead end. Mostly, after being reunited with our pets, Nathan and I will bask in the California sunshine. He'll design wine and beer bottle labels, and I'll be pruning my grape vines."

"Sounds idyllic. We need to come visit you sometime in the winter," Matthew said.

"Come anytime. We have good wine, good food, and good pets," Nathan said. "We probably need to leave for the airport soon as we have to drop the rental off, which will take a little more time. Thanks for hosting us over the holidays."

Hugs and goodbyes were exchanged, luggage was loaded into the car, and they were off to the airport. Before they reached the airport, Jill checked in on the case to see if any new data had arrived on Logan Web. She was just going through that when her cell phone rang with Detective Van Lanen's number.

"Hello, Detective, what can I do for you?"

"Are you home in California?"

"No, we're driving to the airport at the moment. We'll arrive home between midnight and 1 in the morning your time."

"Oh, it's a long journey with time zone changes. So, we were able to break into the laptop. Or I should say, Agent Stephenson did with a little help from Lea—I think that's her name, from Mr. Klein's company. There's some concerning information on the laptop. The gamemaster appears to be after those of us who worked on this case. You're not mentioned, but I just wanted to give you a heads-up."

"Hopefully, you'll arrest him before he leaves for California to find me. How was the information laid out on the laptop?"

"He added a new way to level up in the game and called out by name my partner and me for that level. He mentioned that other people were involved in the case, but we were the only names he had."

"He or she is one sick person. I hope you're taking steps to protect yourselves."

Nathan took his eyes off the road briefly and gave her a look of concern about the conversation.

"Of course. The department is facing a lot of publicity at the moment about this weird crime, but my partner and I are taking steps to make sure that we detectives and our families are safe. Logan gave our names in the chat function of the game."

"Has the FBI profiled the gamemaster? Is this person like the Wizard of Oz, in that they are a coward behind a curtain, or are they a serious threat?"

"I would call them a serious threat given that they murdered Logan Web. I'll ask the FBI if they've profiled him."

"I'd appreciate any further information about this situation when you have it. Sadly, I've had other criminals attack my property in California, so this isn't my first rodeo. I may have my local police chief reach out to you to understand the gravity of the situation."

"Feel free to share my cell phone number with them. I've got to run; I just wanted to share that piece of worrisome news with you."

"Thank you, Detective," Jill said before the call ended.

"That call sounded concerning," Nathan said as he pulled into the car rental agency close to the airport.

They were tied up with unloading their luggage, signing off on their rental paperwork, and walking into the airport. After giving the airlines their bags and getting through security, they returned to their conversation in an empty area of the airport. They could hear if their gate was called for boarding, but they weren't near anyone to overhear their conversation.

"I guess I'm just mildly concerned as my name simply shows up on an autopsy report. I want to wait and see if Shezmu makes an attack on either the detective or the FBI. Those are the folks at the press conference and their names were broadcast. Still, I'll ask Henrik if he can hack into the game to assure me that the leveling up by killing the detectives doesn't include additional levels."

"You should look through all the public and private reports that you have access to and see if your name is mentioned anywhere, and if it is, does it give our address in California? I'd like to see the gamemaster search for you in Wisconsin."

"That's a great suggestion, Nathan. I'll do a thorough search once we're in the air. I could use the airport's wi-fi, but I'd rather have to do this task just once."

Nathan nodded in agreement and they spoke about what they were planning to do once they arrived home. They heard the overhead announcement about boarding for their flight and were soon seated on the plane. Jill had to wait until they reached the cruising altitude of 10,000 feet before pulling out her laptop to begin checking the details of the case to review if her name was mentioned anywhere besides the autopsy report.

She read the most recent law enforcement reports

that she had access to. She doubted that the gamemaster had access to all of the reports in this case. Granted, if he had the skills to create his horrible video game, perhaps he also had the skills to hack into a law enforcement database. That might be another question for Henrik. Then she watched all of the press conferences about the five original deaths and the last one the previous night. Still, she didn't hear or see reference to her.

"I think we're safe. There's no reference to me in any of these documents. That said, if the gamemaster has hacking abilities and can hack into the Green Bay Police Department, then I might be screwed," Jill said to Nathan.

"Sadly, my money is on the gamemaster. You've been targeted far too many times in the past for your work on one of these cases, including in foreign countries. Despite the fact that you can't find any mention of yourself, I think we should consider you a target for the gamemaster."

"If they do come after me, I think we have some time. I think they would feel the need to make an attempt on the detectives before tackling me as a minor player. Still, when we get home, I'll do an in-depth review of the security cameras to make sure we're well protected. At the very least, it will take them a while to arrive near our home."

Nathan nodded and wrote a mental note to himself to practice their martial arts skills—Jill's Taekwondo and his Hapkido. That way, if she was attacked in the near future, she would be refreshed in her martial arts skills to get out of trouble.

Jill noted an email from the detective with the results of the FBI behavioral analysis evaluation of the gamemaster. She read it through, then shared it with Nathan.

"So, basically, the FBI thinks it is a male and he's a psychopath," Nathan said. "Tell me something I didn't know."

"Yes, I'm likewise unimpressed. It's time to switch gears and think about my vineyard. As I do every year about this time, I ask myself if I'm ready to add the expense of a tasting room."

"I could inquire at the university once the term starts again. Maybe make it a student project for someone in economics and business classes on the way to their degree in winemaking," Nathan suggested. He taught marketing in the enology program at the University of California, Davis, which was the premier university program in the United States. In part, this was due to its close position between the Central Valley wine growing region and Napa Valley. As a state, California was the fourth largest wine producer in the world.

"That sounds like a great idea. Hopefully a student project will take my emotion out of the equation. Let me know if that's a possibility."

It was close to midnight when Nathan parked their car in the garage. The pets were waiting at the door to be greeted as soon as they opened it. Both pets smelled their clothing and were unhappy with the scents of Jo's dog and cat. They soon got over their displeasure and were quick to settle in beside Jill and Nathan in their king bed. It had been a long day for Jill, and she was sound asleep in no time.

CHAPTER 17

$\mathcal{A}$s usual, Jill was up hours before Nathan. Even if she went to bed late, her body naturally woke up early. She started by reviewing her security system. She briefly thought about it when they arrived home last night, but she was just so tired from the long day. All of the cameras were working. She sent an email to the security company that managed her system and asked them to do a check as well.

Next, she opened her email to see if there were any updates on any of the events in Wisconsin. There was a message from the detective that was very concerning. Thankfully, both detectives had moved their families and pets out of their houses before bombs had gone off in their primary bedrooms, causing significant damage to both homes. If they had been asleep at the time, they likely would have died as the bomb was under their beds. Now they would have to relocate while their homes were rebuilt. Likewise, bombs were found under the cars at the hotel the FBI agents were staying at. The bombs had exploded and caused damage to cars and the hotel, but nobody was injured. They were tracking the suspect now. As all the bombs were designed similarly, they concluded that it was all related. Both agencies had a manhunt going on for the suspect. They suspected the gamemaster, but he or she was faceless and unidentifiable at the moment.

She picked up her cell phone and called Henrik. She needed more computer support, which he likely could provide. As she had no idea where he was in the world, she texted him to give her a call at his convenience. She was pleasantly surprised when her phone rang almost immediately.

"I always text you as I know it could be the middle of the night wherever you are around the world."

"It's coming up on four in the afternoon here in Germany. I purposely slow down sales at this time of the year as it's the holidays, and my staff deserve time with their families, not me bothering them for new security system price quotes. I'm at home, but Lea and a few of my company's other most brilliant engineers are on the trail of the gamemaster."

"Excellent, that's what I'm calling about. I assume you heard about the bombings in Green Bay."

"Yes, Agent Stephenson called me with the news and to understand what we were doing next. It seems that he's reached out to his fellow computer geeks within the agency, but he hasn't gotten very far."

"Yes, it appears that this gamemaster might match you or Lea for computer skills. So I reviewed my security system here and I'm having my security company double-check my work. I reviewed the police files and my name is not mentioned except as the medical examiner, so I think that I am safe, especially if he looks in Wisconsin."

"I think you're rather screwed on that, my dear Jill. If you Google yourself, it's quite clear who you are and where you live."

"Darn. If you ever want to set up an obstacle course training site like you have at your home in Germany, can I volunteer my land in California? I'd love to have an extra layer of security, and it would make it easier for my local law enforcement agency. These criminals seem to follow me to my home."

"That's not a bad thought. I'll ask one of my staff members to access your land for that purpose. I'll admit that I'm not sure your state laws would permit such a course, but we'll figure that out. I'm sure that's not why you called, though. What do you need me to do, computer-wise?"

"Regarding the bombs used in Green Bay: what can we do to trace the ingredients? Also, do you have access to any satellites? Can we see the bombs being placed? What can we do to trace the gamemaster's location? I believe they're in North America, most likely the US, given how fast they were able to kill Logan Web, but I sure would like to be able to trace their movements. I don't suppose there's any way you can track where they've logged in by IP address?"

"Wow, that's a lot of computer data requests. It's a good thing that the nerds I hire view your random and strange requests as the Olympics of coding and hacking. I have them already working on all of those requests except the satellite views of the streets where the detectives live."

"You're the best!"

"While I'd love to take credit, it's Lea who deserves it. She loves working on your cases because 'it's so much more exciting and challenging', than the day-to-day work she does for my company. So in a roundabout way, your computer requests are what's keeping my workforce engaged with their daily boring work."

"From the mouths of babes," Jill said with a laugh. "I like to think of your company as digitally guarding my six, as police officers say."

"That's a nice way of putting it. If only I could design a forcefield to put over your vineyard."

"Yeah, and maybe all the bad guys after me could go after each other outside the forcefield. Ah, what a fantasy!"

"My company is good, but not that good to create something like that. I'll let you know when we make some headway here with your gamemaster."

"Thanks, Henrik. Appreciate it."

They ended their call, and meanwhile emails were piling up in her inbox. She started with the easy stuff. The Milwaukee Medical Examiner signed off on her version of Logan Web's autopsy. A few more lab tests flowed in, but none helped narrow the window for his time of death. The detective sent her a report about the bombs as an FYI to share with her local law enforcement agency. Jo said the mood of the neighbors was one of happiness that the killer who left bodies in their neighborhood was now dead. Jo said she didn't tell them that there might be a gamemaster out there still targeting people. Finally, there was an email from her security company, and it was concerning.

Sometime over the previous night, her software had undergone an update that was not a part of their company. They were trying to figure out what the update did and where it came from. Other than that, the system was working. She sighed and asked herself, *couldn't she have at least one case where someone involved in the case didn't take revenge on her or her property?*

Nathan came downstairs and must have heard her sigh, so he asked, "What was that sigh for? It must be something about the Wisconsin case."

"I'm amazed you're awake and talking with me this early; as it's not even nine in the morning."

"It's the time zone change. I'll be back on California time in a day or two. So what was the sigh for?"

"I think the gamemaster is probably coming after me. He bombed both detectives' houses as well as the agents' cars. No one was hurt, but the cars are destroyed, and the houses need extensive repairs."

"I have work to do this morning, but first I wanted to do a workout with you to refresh your Taekwondo skills. With this gamemaster after you, it wouldn't hurt to brush up on your martial arts competence," Nathan said.

"I don't disagree with you. Why don't you grab some coffee and breakfast first? I need to call the local police chief and discuss what's going on with this case. They'll likely increase patrols."

"Good idea. I'll do as you suggest. Let me know when you're ready."

She nodded and returned to reading her email. She collected the detective's notes and her security company notes and sent them to the chief, then she picked up the phone to call their non-emergency number. She lucked out and was transferred to the chief.

"Hello, Chief. How are you?"

"It depends on what you're about to tell me. It's never something easy or straight, and it usually strains the resources of my department."

"I just sent you an email that contains a summary of a case I was involved in in Green Bay, Wisconsin. Basically, six people are dead because this horrible person designed a video game that requires players to kill people to level up in the game. The gamemaster who designed this monstrous game just blew up the bedrooms of two detectives and the cars of two FBI agents with whom I worked on the case. We don't know if I'm on the gamemaster's kill list, but given how fast things unfolded in Green Bay, I'm not taking any chances. Also, I spoke with my security company and they're following up on my system. It seems that it went through a software update last night and none of their other systems did, so the gamemaster, who is a computer expert may already have me in the crosshairs."

"What did I tell you, Dr. Quint? You always have some weird case and you'll likely need the resources of my department."

"Yes, but think about how famous you'll be when you arrest the mastermind behind a monstrous video game."

"Yea, right," the chief mumbled. "I'll read the stuff you just sent me and brief the department on the issue."

"Thank you, Chief."

Jill ended that call, then went upstairs to change into her dobok, which is the uniform of Taekwondo. As Nathan's martial art of Hapkido was also Korean in nature, he also wore a dobok, though of a different design from hers. They went outside to one of Jill's outbuildings that they had set up as a dojo, or space to practice martial arts. After stretching, Nathan went on the attack at Jill, forcing her to quickly remember her moves as a brown belt martial artist. She hadn't practiced in a few weeks, and it showed. She was glad Nathan made her practice as she started sluggishly but then her prior practice came into her muscle memory. Nathan had enough training in Hapkido and other martial arts to make it a very difficult battle for her; he was a master black belt, so she couldn't hope to compete with him.

While they battled, Jill told him about the security system glitch and her conversation with the police chief. Nathan nodded and knew he would stick close to home for a while. One of her barns had analytical equipment that she used to study her grapevines and grapes, but also for running patient samples when she performed a private autopsy for a family. He could use that lab to meet with his clients, or he could reschedule them. The university term didn't start for another two weeks, and maybe he could convince Jill to come with him when he needed to spend overnight in Davis one night a week.

With that settled in his mind, even as he was going through martial arts moves with Jill, another part of his brain was devoted to thinking about how to keep her safe when she was out pruning her grapevines. She had acres of vines that she personally tended. She wouldn't hire that out as she considered that step crucial to the success of her wines. He had no answer to that critical question, but maybe she could stay away from the vineyard for a week, and in that time, law enforcement would find the gamemaster and arrest him.

"I presume you spoke with Henrik, and I know you spoke with the chief of police. Have you contacted Leticia Ortiz yet?" Nathan asked. She was the FBI Special Agent in Charge of the San Francisco office, and she had helped Jill on other cases, just as Jill had assisted the agent.

"Actually, that's a good idea. I hadn't thought to call her as the Midwest FBI is already on the case. I'll call her as soon as we're done here to see if she has any suggestions we haven't considered yet."

"I hope you'll walk around the property with pepper spray—just be prepared for this gamemaster to come after you. The fact that they boldly bombed the detectives' houses and the agents' cars means this person has no limits. I want to check in with Henrik to see what he's discovered. I'm really worried about this psychopath coming after you."

"I know. I feel uneasy about it too. I thought about running away—hop aboard a plane and get away—but at least here I know the law enforcement folks and they know me. It's such a crazy story that I would likely have a hard time convincing the police in small-town Portugal that a video gamemaster was trying to kill me."

"That's probably true. We need to get some help here defending our castle, our pets, and ourselves."

"Yes, I gave a few moments of thought to one of my early cases. It was just as we were starting to date. The FBI had put me up in their headquarters building in San Francisco. The bad guys even tried to take me out there." Then Jill had an idea and said, "Remind me to call Damian Green when we return to the house."

Nathan looked puzzled at the name but nodded. They finished their workout and headed to the house.

Jill called Leticia and was put into her voicemail, so she left a message about the case. Then she called Damian Green and she again ended up in voicemail so she also left a message about the case.

"Who's Damian Green?" Nathan asked.

"He's the only guy I've met who gives Henrik competition in the geek department. He lives on an island in San Francisco Bay called Red Rock Island. His home there is very well fortified and he has fought off as many terrible criminals as I have. He has water cannons and drones that drop dye on any intruder approaching his island by boat. I wonder if he would lend us his house until the gamemaster is caught? Or maybe he can figure out the identity of this horrible human being is."

"That's a pretty big ask to have him give up his house for us."

"I'll see what he says. Maybe he can set up some defenses for our property as I seem to be attacked frequently."

Her phone rang and the caller ID said it was Damian Green. She put the phone on speaker and answered it.

"Hi Damian, Jill Quint here. I hope you remember who I am."

"I do. You're the forensic pathologist friend of Leticia Ortiz and you have a friend who is a computer whiz whom I should meet some day."

"Exactly. My friend's name is Henrik Klein and he's based in Germany. He's been working on a case for me and I need more help. Let me explain the case," Jill said and described what had happened in Green Bay and what they had discovered about the gamemaster so far.

"Wow. So you would like me to find the gamemaster's identity?"

"Yes. I also have a bigger ask—I wondered if I could borrow your house."

"Excuse me?" Damian said.

"Given that the gamemaster got inside two detectives' homes to plant bombs, I'm feeling very vulnerable in my vineyard. There's just too much open land to defend. Also, my security company said that my system had undergone a software update, yet their company had not scheduled any updates. So I'm worried that this sick gamemaster has gotten into my cameras and can turn the alarms off."

"I understand your concern. My girlfriend, Ariana, and our charge live in Belvedere and I could move there for a week until this gamemaster is caught. I'll do a head-to-head competition with your techy friend Henrik to find out who can find the gamemaster first. Let me think this over as I've never, in almost a decade, had a stranger stay here, let alone take over the house, but I get your concern. Is it just you?"

"No. I would come with my husband, Nathan, and our cat and dog. Neither animal will cause damage to your property."

"I have two cats that are used to being fed fresh fish from the bay. Can you continue that duty?"

"Nathan can do that."

"Okay, I'll call you back."

They ended the call and Jill bet that Damian was checking out her story with all of his sources.

"You volunteered me for fishing duty?" Nathan asked.

"I did. Do you know how to fish?"

"Not really, but I can learn. Arthur may never want to come home if he gets to eat fresh fish twice daily."

"Fingers crossed that we could move there. We would be impossible to find. I'll admit this is a huge favor to ask of this guy, but I think he's sympathetic to my situation as his first family was murdered by a mistakenly released prisoner, so we'll see. I'm going to hop into the shower; can you watch my phone in case he calls back?"

Nathan nodded and Jill was soon showered and changed and making mental notes of what she would take with her if they moved to the island. It was a little less than two hours away, depending on traffic. She returned to the living room and soon figured out that Nathan was on the phone with Leticia Ortiz.

"Here's Jill now, just a moment."

"Hi Leticia. You got my message?"

"Trust you to be involved in one of the weirdest cases ever. I knew about the happenings in Wisconsin as all the FBI offices were informed. What I didn't know was that you were at the center of it."

"Yes, well, the victims' remains were placed in a house around the corner from Jo Pringle's house, so the team and I were working to make her neighborhood safer."

"Ah, that makes sense now. What do you need from me?"

"I called Damian Green to see if he would give up his island home for Nathan and me. I feel very vulnerable on my acres of vineyard, and considering the gamemaster had the cojones to bomb the detectives' houses, I figure I might be next as well, as my good friend Henrik. If Damian doesn't want to give up his home for us—and that is a big request, then do you have agents you can assign to my property? The gamemaster likely has already been into my security system."

"How do you know that?" Leticia asked.

"As soon as I arrived back from Wisconsin, I called my security company and asked them to check my system to make sure it was functioning as it should. They discovered an unauthorized software update that they're trying to run down. I'm suspicious that the gamemaster who is an expert at coding, has access to my cameras and can turn them off at any moment, which would make me blind to what they were up to."

"Okay. Let me do some research on my end. It sounds like you have the two best computer experts on your side trying to run down this gamemaster. I doubt the FBI will be faster than your resources."

"Thanks, Leticia," Jill said, just as she saw an incoming call from Damian Green.

"Hi Damian, I just got off the phone with Leticia Ortiz," Jill said, knowing that he knew who she was from his work with her on separate law enforcement cases.

"Is she going to supply you with protection?" Damian asked.

"Not yet."

"Okay, well then it's your lucky day. You can pack up your pets and yourselves and have my house for a week. Between you, your friend, and me, we should have this case resolved by then. How soon can you be here?"

"Give me thirty minutes to wrap up here and then

it's less than a two-hour drive to San Francisco. Where should we meet you? I presume a boat is the only way to reach your island."

"That's correct. As it is the weekend, I'm at home at the moment. Meet me at the Richmond Marina," he gave her the address and she promised to text him when they hit the city of Richmond so he could boat over. He also reminded them to bring food of their choosing as they would be stuck on the island until he returned with his boat. She added another thirty minutes to their arrival to do grocery shopping.

Eventually Nathan and Jill, with pets and supplies for a week, arrived at the Richmond Marina to find a pontoon boat with Damian Green at the helm. Jill performed introductions and they loaded their supplies, luggage, and pets and were soon crossing the bay to the island. Jill had never noticed the island the few times she had driven over the Richmond-San Rafael bridge. It was a short journey and Damian pulled into his dock. They were met by a teenager, introduced as Hermione, who helped tie down the boat and then unload and carry supplies inside and upstairs to the living space.

Hermione looked like a high school junior or senior and was introduced as Damian's ward. She had brought Damian's friend's boat over as he didn't have a boat large enough to fit the two adults, their belongings, and their pets. She was also there to train Nathan on how to use the island's protections. Meanwhile Jill was given an orientation to the island, the house, and the down-stairs lab.

"I would appreciate it if you would stay out of the downstairs unless the island is under attack and you need the computers to fire at intruders. Know that I can also access the defensive equipment and take over any battle remotely. The walls of the house are bullet-proof so even if someone arrived by helicopter with an automatic weapon, the house will stand against that assault. Members of the Arian Brotherhood fired on the house and they were not able to damage it."

"Your life sounds as treacherous as mine is at times. How do I add this stuff to my house? I feel bad calling on you for protection."

"We'll look at that after this gamemaster is caught. I put some protections around my girlfriend's house and could add some of that for you."

They were standing outside on the top of the island, and as Jill watched, water cannons fired from the rocky cliff above a small beach. Then she heard drones over-head and watched as one dropped a brightly colored balloon onto the sand. The drone operator had dropped the water balloon at the water's edge, and the waves were already dissolving the dye.

"Hermione's showing your husband how to operate the water cannons and the drones. Those balloons have an acid solution that is bright green. It stains the skin of anyone it hits and carries microcrystals to make them easy to track. It also blinds some intruders for up to eight hours."

"Wow, when I asked to use your house, I had no idea how well protected I would be. At least I'll be able to sleep at night."

"Yes, as you might know my wife and our two daughters were murdered by a convict who was mistakenly released from Soledad Prison. I now have a monitoring system in place to make sure the prison never makes that mistake again, and I built my defenses with the thought of holding off criminals. Never again."

Jill put her hand on his coat sleeve and said, "I'm so sorry for your loss and congratulations on rebuilding your life. You seem to be raising Hermione well, and I'm sure that heals a small part of your broken heart."

"It does. Someday I might tell you her courageous story, but not today."

Trixie had been exploring the island, and the door opened and Nathan and Arthur stepped out with Hermione behind them. Arthur sauntered over to the cliff and began exploring.

Nathan asked, "Where's your fishing pole and what's your process for feeding your cats?"

Damian asked Hermione to grab his pole, which he kept behind the front door. He then showed Nathan his favorite fishing spot and how to find worms for his hook. In no time at all, he pulled in a small fish. He and Nathan went inside so Nathan could understand what the cats were used to in terms of fish food.

Jill held her hand out to Hermione and said, "I heard you're Damian's ward. Thanks for showing my husband how to work the island's defenses."

"I've helped Damian defeat bad people trying to take over this island. It's actually a lot of fun to aim those water cannons at intruders. They don't die, but it's a cold boat ride back to wherever they came from if the police don't capture them first. I heard you're a forensic pathologist," the teenager said, slowing her words down to pronounce them correctly.

"I am. I'm a physician who decided in medical school that I enjoyed helping law enforcement take down criminals. I also like to show respect to the dead by giving them their final physical exam. It's my duty to make sure that I identify any suspicious circumstance that might make a death look like something it's not. For example, I just did a private consultation and autopsy in Green Bay, Wisconsin, because their medical examiner was off for the holiday. That man's death was made to look like a suicide, but it was a homicide."

"I've been accepted to UC Berkeley in the fall, and I was thinking of doing pre-med. I haven't figured out what interests me yet as a doctor. Perhaps when you're no longer being threatened, I could spend some time with you to understand your training and what you do."

"I'd love to host you and talk about my field. I'm also sub-boarded in toxicology, so we can talk about poisons as well. I also operate a winery in the Central Valley, and I have a chemistry lab in one of my barns."

"I can't wait to take a tour. How far a drive is it?"

"If you're leaving from Richmond, it's just under two hours. I'm not sure about coming from Belvedere."

"I'll figure it out. Give me your contact information

so we can make arrangements at a later date," Hermione said, and they traded cell numbers and then turned and entered the house.

Before the door Trixie could close slipped inside. She was in a strange place and wanted to stay close to her humans.

"Damian, might we get locked outside of the house?" Jill asked, not seeing a doorknob on the front door.

"You shouldn't. My doors unlock with facial recognition, and I entered your faces into the system. Are you comfortable with the technology in my home?"

"I am. I do need wi-fi access as I run a business as a wine and beer label artist, and I'll have to move my clients to video conferencing for this coming week," Nathan said.

"You two have such interesting occupations. Maybe when I come to visit Dr. Quint, you could show me what you do also," Hermione said to Nathan.

"Of course. I teach at UC Davis, so you'll just be another student," Nathan said.

"Cool. We'd better get going, Damian; Ariana was starting dinner when I left."

"Well, folks, you have my number if you need anything, and I would appreciate it if you would stay out of the lower level as I have fragile equipment down there," Damian said just before he and Hermione exited to the stairs that would take them to the dock.

Jill and Nathan waved them off. When they saw the dock fold up into the side of the island thanks to a video camera, Nathan said, "You sure have some interesting friends. This island is a small fortress. We are totally safe here, and even if the gamemaster finds us, we'll nail him with eye-stinging green goo and it will be easier for the cops to find him."

"I knew that his house was high tech as he is like Henrik. Just think of the toys he has at his house. I asked him to install some of this at our house once this case is over. He said he upgraded his girlfriend's house with stuff, so I think he could help us. Are you going to be able to handle the fishing?"

"Yes. He's a smart guy and he figured out pretty quickly that I didn't know anything about fishing. Now I know how to feed his cats and what fish parts to cut up and what to discard. If I should fail to find a fish, he told me where the dry kibble is."

"He's been so generous that we can't fail his cats. Where are they, by the way?"

"They're asleep on his bed. He said he didn't want to disrupt their sleep, so he showed me where the clean sheets are so I can make the bed once they go out for the night. Apparently, unless it is raining, they like to hunt at night. That reminds me: I should bring Arthur inside and introduce them."

"What are their names?" Jill asked as Nathan went to the door to get Arthur to come inside.

Arthur came trotting in and Nathan picked him up and said, "Bella and Bailey. Hermione said there's also a dog named Miguel that visits the island on occasion, so there probably are dog smells for Trixie to explore."

Jill followed Nathan into the bedroom to meet the

cats and check out the room. It was a small house created for a single guy, but it had everything they needed—a bed, bathroom, kitchen, and living room with a television. Most importantly, they were safe from a stone-cold killer.

Arthur acknowledged the two cats and then returned to the living room. Trixie tried to smell their butts and got scratched for her over-familiar behavior, so she also left for the living room. The cats settled back to sleep and the two humans left the bedroom as well.

They unpacked their food and supplies and then sat down on the sofa. Jill wanted to catch up on the latest news about finding the gamemaster. There were no additional bombings in Green Bay, so where did the gamemaster go next to exact his revenge?

Jill took the time to bring Henrik up to date on what was going on and a heads-up that she soon would be introducing him to Damian Green, who she told him was the other computer genius in her life. Introductions soon were performed via text and email; she'll let the two computer geniuses compete on who could solve the case faster.

Then she saw a concerning email.

This was her security system sending her pings of someone stepping on her property. She looked at the time and it was about thirty minutes after they had left their home. The figure wore bulky clothing such that you couldn't tell whether it was a man or woman. The figure had a mask on. She viewed the footage a few times to see if there were any good shots of the intruder, but there were none. Then her system went down for about half an hour before coming back up. What happened on her property in those thirty minutes?

"Our security system went down for about thirty minutes. I don't know about you, but I find this gamemaster scary because I know they're on a computer genius level like Henrik. I wonder if I can get an explosive sniffing dog in? I doubt our small town has such a dog."

"We're not there now, but if he's timed it to go off in the middle of the night, that will damage our house. Let's get a dog in to see if a bomb can be found and deactivated."

"I'll call the chief." She did, and fortunately he knew the situation well enough to take her request seriously. He called her back with the news that Lodi was sending their bomb crew to Jill's house. They would be there in less than an hour, and the chief had shared with Lodi police the explosives report from the Green Bay detectives.

She relayed this news to Nathan, who was figuring out his workflow for the coming week if he was to stay on Red Rock Island. He had one client whom he needed to meet with in person, and he would bet that he could hitch a ride to the Richmond Marina when Damian was crossing the bay to reach his offices in Richmond. Nathan could then take his car to Napa Valley, which was less than an hour away. The gamemaster was after Jill, not Nathan so even if he somehow figured out where they had gone, he wasn't going to follow Nathan to Napa.

Jill received texts from Damian and Henrik that sounded promising. Damian might have the edge on the locations of the gamemaster when he was logged in. Damian knew more about satellites and computing clouds, while Henrik was the king of facial and object recognition. Henrik had worked on the images from her vineyard and Damian was chasing the IP address of all the gamers' logins. The bad news was that when

Damian traced the Green Bay and California logins, he discovered one that was very close to her vineyard. Somehow the gamemaster must have figured out that Jill was involved in bringing Henrik into the case and that he had discovered their entire monstrous video game.

Jill heaved a sigh.

Nathan looked over at her and said, "That was a deep sigh. Just remember, the house is replaceable, but we're not. We are safe here, as are our pets. Let's think of something else for a moment. What should we give Damian to thank him for the use of his home?"

"He's a millionaire, right? So he can buy whatever he wants."

"So let's give him our time and expertise. We'll spend time with his ward and we can go a step further and arrange for her to meet anyone else connected to our jobs if she wants. So if she wants to see an autopsy, you'll escort her to whatever medical examiner's office she wants to visit. Likewise, if Damian wants an assessment of a winery for purchase, I'll assist him in that or even just choosing wine for his home. I don't see a wine refrigerator unless it's in the basement and I'm not going to violate his privacy and look."

"Those are great ideas. We'll definitely talk about that with him when we give the house back to him. Thanks for that diversion from worrying about our house being blown up."

Nathan leaned over to hug Jill.

She was waiting for news from Henrik, Damian,

and her local police chief. The waiting was frustrating her to no end.

"Let's go outside and fish. The wait for new information is driving me nuts."

Nathan nodded. Compared to Wisconsin, California was downright balmy, but the bay could be damp and windy so after they grabbed their coats, and Arthur and Trixie followed them outside. With a fishing pole in hand, Nathan settled on the rocks on the short side of the cliffs surrounding the island. He dug a little in the soil near them for a worm and put it on the hook. Then he cast out into the water. A short time later, he was reeling in a fish. The cat and dog were fascinated by the wiggling creature that Nathan dropped into the bucket of water he brought with him. He baited the hook and gave it to Jill to cast.

"We're pretty pathetic in that we don't know the basics of fishing," Jill said.

"Yes, well, we know lots of other things. People just shouldn't count on us if Armageddon has happened and we need to fish or hunt to eat."

She fist bumped Nathan and was then pleasantly surprised when she felt a tug on the fishing pole. She started slowly reeling in the fishing line and found a wiggling fish on the end of it, which she handed over to Nathan.

He removed the fish from the line and said, "We have enough for Bella and Bailey. Should we fish for our two pets now?"

It was an interesting diversion. The day was cloudy

and windy. It was about 50 degrees Fahrenheit before the wind was calculated in.

"This is a really peaceful place. I can see why Damian retreated here—you're smack in the middle of the Bay Area and yet not a soul can touch you on this island," Jill said.

"Yes. While your vineyard is a very relaxing place, it feels very vulnerable when one of your criminals is up to no good."

"Yes. I wonder if the bomb squad has arrived yet?"

"Let's go inside and look at the cameras on the property to find out."

"That's an excellent idea. Should we catch one more fish for our pets?"

Nathan looked at the fish swimming around in the bucket and thought of Damian's instructions and said, "We have enough for all four animals." They packed up and went back inside the house.

While Nathan chopped up the fish for later, Jill opened her laptop and pulled up views from her security system. There were multiple cars in their driveway, and she could tell that some of them were police cars. She'd given the police the alarm code to the house so they could enter. There was a man in a big puffy suit that reminded Jill of Buzz Lightyear from the *Toy Story* movie. He must be the bomb technician. Jill saw him disappear inside the house. He returned less than two minutes later; Jill guessed he had found something. She had audio and video in her security system, but their conversations were too far away for her to hear clearly.

"Something is going on at the house. Buzz Lightyear went in and out of our house in about two minutes," Jill said to Nathan. She put her laptop on the coffee table in front of them, so they both could watch.

"Buzz Lightyear?"

"I think the dude in the bomb suit sort of looks like the character from the Disney movie."

Nathan couldn't remember seeing the movie, so he did a quick search on his phone. Jill was right; the guy looked like Buzz. Despite the protective suit, that was a scary occupation.

Jill texted the chief, who was onsite at the house, for details. He must have felt the vibration of her text as she watched him pull his phone out of a pocket and read something which she hoped was her text. She watched him type something on the phone, and then heard the ding of her phone.

She checked and indeed, it was a text from him. It said, *Bomb found under your bed. Additional resources are on their way. We would send in a robot, but it can't reach the location.*

"Oh my gosh! There's a bomb under our bed," Jill told Nathan as she shared the text from the chief with him. "I'll let Damian know that he might have saved our lives today."

"You saved our lives when you thought of asking for his help with the gamemaster and to give us a safe place to hide out."

Jill waved away his comment, intent on writing a text to Damian and to the chief. After she hit send on both, she looked up and said, "Thank you for staying with me through thick and thin on these cases. I'm sorry I put your life in danger."

It was his turn to wave away the words and then he leaned in to kiss her. She heard a double ding suggesting two arriving texts. She looked at her phone and Damian had said, *"Glad I could help.*

The chief's message indicated that the bomb was due to go off in about nine hours—exactly when they would have been asleep.

"What an evil man," Nathan commented. "He's willing to kill a man and woman and their pets, and that's after he killed Logan Web, who he in turn had killed five people following this evil man's directions."

"Yes, he's pretty evil. I wonder what he's doing now. Is he staying in the area near the house waiting for it to explode? I don't think so since he didn't stick around for the two detectives and agents to see if his bombs killed them."

"Or maybe he's such a narcissist that he can't imagine that his bombs might fail to kill his targets," Nathan suggested.

"Maybe. It would be great for the house if the bomb doesn't explode, and it would be even better if the gamemaster left fingerprints on the device."

An email arrived that was addressed to Jill and Henrik from Damian. He had accessed satellites that had their eyes on Jill's property as well as the detectives' homes in Green Bay. He was able to get a decent facial image of their bomber before he pulled the mask up over his face. Damian thought it was a male. Now it was up to Henrik to identify him.

She waited a few minutes for Henrik to respond with the identity of their gamemaster. Jill wished she was sitting next to Damian or Henrik as they closed in on this evil genius. Nathan was watching the video feed of their house, while Jill looked at her phone for a new email.

Nathan murmured, "Additional resources from Sacramento are arriving."

Jill looked up and nodded. Then she saw a new text from Henrik. They had the name of the gamemaster. It was Devin Vale. Henrik also supplied a few facts about him, including his age and last-known address. She forwarded the name of the gamemaster to Marie for her to work her magic and then asked Henrik and Damian for information about their suspect. She also sent Agent Ortiz a text updating her on, what was going on as well as the chief. She sent the chief images taken from the roads, and he said he would immediately issue an Attempt To Locate notice with his picture.

That taken care of, Jill started her own search on Devin Vale is, but first she said to Nathan, "We have the name of the gamemaster. It's Devin Vale. I don't know more than that, but I'm sure that in under an hour we'll know a lot as Henrik, Damian, and Marie are all searching for information about him."

"That's great news. Protecting ourselves from a

faceless, nameless enemy just got easier. I'll see what I can find also."

It was quiet in the house except for the clacking of keys, not just because it was literally on an island, but because they all raced to find information about Devin Vale. A short time later, Jill knew lots of information about their suspect. He lived in Chicago and until recently had been a professor of psychology and computer science at a major university there. He was an expert in the gamification of behavior. He was fired for conducting unprofessional psychology studies on students without their knowledge or consent. It was quite a scandal at the school. It seemed that he had created a video game in addition to Murder-Rage and encouraged the students to play the game. The students had no idea that he was manipulating them as the gamemaster until they got together and then went to complain to the university's leadership. Sadly, the investigation revealed that two students had died by suicide due to his manipulation game.

When Devin was hired, the school called him a generational talent in computer science and psychology. As a graduate student, he had published a paper about manipulating minds with video games. Little did the university know that he continued his work in secret by creating a new game and encouraging his students to play it. It was only when the second student ended their life that the students realized that something was off. Things went quickly after that, and within a month he was fired and no university wanted to hire him.

Jill wondered where his funding came from if he was no longer a professor. She sent that question to Jo and Matthew. She also looked into his background to understand how he knew explosives. From what she could tell, he was self-taught, which probably wasn't surprising given his IQ, which was high. Still, Jill was smart, and yet she would never consider playing with explosives or learning by video, but to each his own when it came to risks. Now the question was: where was he and how did they go about finding him? Then she thought about how he had found her—Devin must have hacked into the police records to find her name, and she wondered what Damian or Henrik could do to chase down how he was logging in. She sent a note to both of them.

She returned to watching the video of their house. She hoped that the guy couldn't set off the bomb remotely and that they really did have some eight hours to save her house. They watched as a big van pulled into her driveway with the words FBI Bomb Squad written on the side. It looked like additional resources had arrived. Nathan and Jill continued to watch the activity at their house, wondering if there even would be a house standing at the end of the night. After an intense hour of hoping their house would survive and no one would be injured, they both heaved sighs of relief when they saw something brought out of the house and then the package was purposely exploded a short time later.

"Whew," Nathan said, sighing. Then he tensed again as he saw another bomb squad member enter their house with a dog.

"Don't let the dog get hurt," Jill whispered at the screen.

She was tense until she saw the dog and its handler return outside about twenty minutes later. It looked like they gave the all-clear. Hopefully their house was cleared of any bombs. Now she just had to worry about Devin Vale returning and planting a new bomb.

"That was exhausting to watch," Nathan said.

"I know. Kudos to the men and women who sign up for bomb squad duty. I don't think I could do that," Jill said.

"Me either," Nathan said. "My biggest danger is being fired by a vineyard owner if they don't like my label design."

"Hey, you're brave. Look at the times you've gone to bat for me and taken on the bad criminals."

"Yes, but that's instinct. I don't volunteer for that duty. I just have to respond when you're in danger."

"Yes, but your instinct could be to run and instead you stay and defend me," Jill said, leaning in to give him a kiss of gratitude and love, then she added, "We're getting sappy here."

"Yes, it must be the deserted island influencing us, or maybe it's the relief of not having our house blown up."

She heard another ding from her phone and looked to find a message from Damian. It was good news. He had managed to isolate the phone or laptop that Devin Vale was using and now he could track him. Damian searched for someone who had hacked into the police records to find Jill's name and then took it from there. Devin was presently on Interstate 80 outside of Reno, Nevada, presumably heading to his home in Chicago. Damian had been able to take an overhead picture of the vehicles on the freeway while triangulating Devin's phone. It was one of six vehicles in the picture. However, it most likely was one of five, and the sixth was a semi-tractor trailer.

She texted him back to see if he had shared the picture with Leticia Ortiz. He hadn't but he would now.

Nathan had been following the conversation and said, "It seems like we can return home in the morning. Our house is cleared of bombs and the suspect is more than five hundred miles away."

"Maybe. We need law enforcement to run down those six vehicles and make sure Vale is in one of them and that he didn't just throw his phone into one of the vehicles."

"You think he's that sneaky?" Nathan asked.

"Remember, Devin Vale has a mensa-level IQ. Of course, that doesn't always calculate to common sense or strategic thinking."

"True that."

Eventually, they received a call from the chief that their house was clear of all bombs. Meanwhile, a helicopter and small plane were launched from the Reno branch of the FBI to run down the five cars and the semi. Two Nevada Highway Patrol cars were dispatched to assist with a freeway stop. Whatever law enforcement found with this freeway stop would determine if Jill and Nathan could move back home.

Nathan was preparing dinner while Jill continued to monitor the Nevada situation. Damian had sent her a link so she could watch the tracking live. The phone came to a stop, so now it was a matter of waiting to see if Devin Vale was in one of the vehicles.

A half-hour later, after all six vehicles were searched, there was no Devin Vale. The phone was found duck-taped to the back underside of the semitruck.

"Darn, we can't go home. They didn't find Devin Vale. He taped his phone to the semitruck. I wonder where he really is at the moment?" Jill asked.

CHAPTER 20

Devin Vale was frustrated. In his mind, he was a brilliant scientist who created a video game that allowed him to control other people through psychological manipulation. His crowning achievement was when others killed for him. It was the ultimate control of another human being. He didn't do it through threats; rather, he did it through gamification, and he was dying to share his findings with the academic world.

He'd designed his first video game five years ago and sold it to a major video game distributor. As long as he managed his finances and didn't get reckless in his spending, he never needed to work again. Those stupid fools at the university were lucky he hadn't blown them up. While he wasn't excited about losing his job, he was pleased to have more time to work on video games. He had been thinking about designing Murder-Rage as a way to explore the boundaries of what you could do with gamification, which was using points, leaderboards, and badges to improve user engagement and motivation.

The game was going really well until Dr. Jill Quint brought her computer expert into the situation, and he successfully hacked his way into Devin's video game. Now he couldn't sell this technology to anyone as it had such a bad reputation. Still, he could hide out for a year or two and then create a new game. Companies would love to influence consumer buying behavior, and the fact that he proved he could influence human behavior enough to make people kill one another surely demonstrated his key hypothesis about video games and human behavior.

Now the other thing in his way was this forensic pathologist and her computer friend, a Henrik Klein from Germany. She brought him into the murders by BadSpider5, and then the German guy's staff had hacked into his game and he had to shut it down. He wasn't an indecisive person, but he didn't know if he should stay in California and get rid of the doctor first and then head to Germany to take care of her friend, or the reverse. He knew how to get explosives in America, but he would have to find a new supply of them in Europe. If she didn't have this Henrik Klein helping her, then his video game would have remained undiscovered by the authorities.

He decided that he needed to know what the cops knew, something he couldn't be bothered with paying attention to. He did a little research and he was furious. The cops in Wisconsin hadn't died, nor had the agents. Then he hacked into the doctor's security cameras and hit the remote detonator that he had left inside her house. He knew he might not kill her as it was daytime and it was unlikely she would be in her bedroom, or indeed in her house at all, but he could scare her, which would have to do.

Nothing happened. No explosion. He hit the button again. Again, nothing happened. He scanned the older video to see what had occurred since he had left her property, and then he saw what happened—a bomb squad had been called and they'd removed the explosives from her house. How did she know they were there? Was it a lucky guess or had he left evidence behind?

He thought to look something else up and was devastated by the search. The police had his name and a picture, and there was a manhunt for him at the moment. How did she find his identity? He hadn't worn clothing that revealed his face when on her property. Then he realized his mistake. Devin hadn't put his mask on until he got close to the property. She and her computer experts must have pulled his image from a mile or two away from her property. He had gotten cocky and assumed the only cameras he needed to worry about were those that were on her property. There must have been additional cameras that captured his image. Now he knew his priority had to be to kill the doctor first, as it would be difficult to travel internationally without some extra work like a new passport or slipping across the border into Mexico. Thank goodness he had a reminder on his calendar to change out his main phone every month, or he might have been caught. He always taped it to the bottom of a semi-tractor trailer whenever he switched phones. He used tape and stuck the phones where they would get the wash from the wheels, knowing that the tape would come loose and drop the phone somewhere where it could be crushed by another vehicle.

Well, two could play at that game. He would follow her on satellite and he would see where she had gone. He could blow her up in her new location. He would find her. She'd hurt his immediate financial future, and he needed to take care of her before she could do any more damage. Her death was critical to the future success that he had planned out in his brain.

Devin pulled up the footage on her security system to get an image of her car and its license plate. Then he hacked into the highway cameras. He really was great with computers, something the university had never appreciated. He bet that in a head-to-head competition, he would crush this Henrik Klein. He downloaded the various live cameras databases and searched for the car.

Jill Quint and the man with her drove toward San Francisco. Were they going to stay somewhere in San Francisco or fly somewhere? He frowned as he watched her get off the freeway well short of San Francisco or its airport, or even the nearby airport of Oakland. Did she have a friend in Richmond? He switched from the highway cameras to the city cameras. It was hard to find her on the city cameras as only a few streets had cameras. He looked at the camera on the Richmond San Rafael bridge but didn't see her car. Where did she go?

It took him another couple of hours, but he eventually followed her to the marina, and her car was still parked there. He thought about putting a bomb on her car, but without knowing when she would return to the car, that seemed like a mediocre plan. Instead, he went to the website that offered tracking of boats on San Francisco Bay and what he saw astounded him.

Dr. Quint didn't go very far in the boat. She stopped at Red Rock Island, which was a mere mile or so beyond the marina. He pulled up satellite images to see what was on the island and it appeared to be a house. Then he tried to figure out who owned the island, but he ran into a dead end. Whoever owned it did an awesome job of hiding their identity. Maybe her computer friend Henrik owned it and had hidden his name well.

Then he pulled up a topographical map of the island to see where he could attack it. He also looked at the marinas near the island. While Richmond was the closest, there were also marinas all over the bay where he could rent a boat to reach the island. With a plan in mind, he checked out of his hotel and made the drive northwest to Jill Quint, who as far as he was concerned was a sitting duck on that island in the bay.

CHAPTER 21

Damian Green was a brilliant computer genius, and he protected his privacy in fiendishly clever ways. He had alerts whenever Red Rock Island or he himself was mentioned in the news, or when someone searched for his property or his name. He got an alert that an IP address was looking up the ownership records for his island. He got those alerts about once every couple of months, and just now he had one. With Jill and Nathan on his island, was this about them or just some random curious person looking things up on the internet? He knew that Devin Vale's phone was not in one of cars in Nevada, so was this him or just a random human? If someone knew how to hack into the highway cameras, it would be fairly easy to follow Jill from her vineyard to his island.

Using his tracking information, he figured that the curious person was traveling toward San Francisco from the Central Valley of California. Devin Vale might have been a brilliant computer nerd, but he was lazy when it came to protecting his cell phone privacy. He picked up his phone and called Jill Quint.

"Hi Damian. What's up?"

"I have tracking notifications on various pieces of information about myself, and I just got an alert that someone was looking into the ownership of Red Rock Island. I then traced that back to a cellular phone that is on the move from the Central Valley toward San Francisco. It might be coincidence or . . ."

"It might be Devin Vale. So, he'll have to rent a boat to reach the island unless he has an inflatable dinghy in his trunk."

"Yes. He's about an hour away, and it will take some time to find a boat. It will be dark by then. I'm going to have Ariana drop Hermione and me off at the island in about an hour if he and the phone continue toward the marina. We're really good at defending the island from intruders. I'll also alert Leticia Ortiz so she can coordinate an arrest if a boat does approach the island. I may be massively over-reacting, but . . ."

"It's better to be safe than sorry," Jill finished for him. "Thank you for being so diligent, and Nathan and I appreciate your help defending your island. If the FBI can swoop in and arrest Devin Vale, then we could get out of your home tonight. We haven't changed the sheets yet as the cats are still sleeping," Jill said with a smile in her voice.

"I appreciate you not disturbing them."

"Of course. I would do the same with my own pets. It would be great to have law enforcement arrest him out on the water rather than trying to locate his car at night on the freeway."

"My thinking exactly. Hopefully, I'll see you soon, as that will mean that Devin Vale is heading for the island."

Jill agreed and ended the call. She'd put the phone on speaker when he called, so Nathan knew the plan.

"That would be cool if this all ended tonight. Besides the danger to ourselves, I had a list of people I'd planned to reschedule for next week. I didn't notify them yet, and it would be nice not to have to."

"Yes, I would love to see Devin Vale detained by law enforcement. He's a narcissist who has lost his ever-loving mind. When I read reviews about him where he was teaching, students described him as smart and eerily quiet but totally lacking in empathy for anything going on in their lives. I would bet that most professors had heard all the excuses for not getting work completed on time by students, but he took it to another level, from what his students said in their reviews."

"He seems to be a genius like Henrik or Damian, but they choose to do good with their intellect, and that doesn't appear to be in Devin's personality," Nathan said.

"No. I feel very lucky to know both men. They're very nice human beings. Fingers crossed that it's Devin coming our way and that Leticia marshals the resources to take him into custody. He won't be able to hurt us here from what I understand of the island, but if he gets away, then that will continue to hang over our heads."

They watched as the sun set, and then she got a text from Damian that they were on their way. Jill considered that a good sign. They had looked at the exterior cameras of the island, but there wasn't much to see in the dark. About fifteen minutes later, they saw a small boat approach. Nathan switched the view to where he knew the dock was, and he saw it fold out from the island's water garage. He saw Damian and Hermione step onto the dock, and then the boat motored away.

Soon the lower-level door opened and Damian and Hermione stepped into the living room. The teenager was smiling. "I love getting to defend Damian's island. It's better than any video game."

"She's just tired of my beating her at Fortnite," Damian said fondly.

The two cats, hearing Damian's voice, apparently decided to wake up as it must be dinner time.

"I fished earlier for the cats, but I haven't cut it up yet. I cut the heads off and threw them off the island, and the remainder of the fish is covered in the refrigerator. I'll feed all four pets if you want to man the battle stations," Nathan said with a grin.

"That sounds like a plan. Jill, you might want to watch and decide if any of my technologies are good for your house."

"After this case is over, you should talk with Henrik. He has an obstacle course outside his house in

Germany. It's so good that it caught a highly trained serial killer who was after us. He even lets the German law enforcement groups train on his course," Jill said. "I'll come watch you take down Devin Vale. I assume you reached Leticia?"

"Yes. She's coordinated with the Coast Guard and she's onboard a Coast Guard cutter as we speak. Once we confirm that he's left a marina on a boat, they'll approach the island. So we need to disable him and prevent him from returning ashore."

"How will you do that?" Nathan asked from where he was cutting the fish in the kitchen.

"We'll need to disable him or his boat. I plan to drop some homemade pepper spray on him once he comes ashore and that will blind him for a while so he won't be able to find his way back to the boat. I was also thinking of once he steps on the island to approach the house, I'll have Hermione distract him while I launch one of my watercrafts. I'd drive it around and board his boat and back it away from the island, before repositioning the anchor."

"This is going to be fun to watch. If you do decide to take out one of your boats, I can help Hermione if she gives me a little instruction on using the equipment."

"I think Damian's defensive systems are like playing one of those huge church organs, where your feet are doing something and there are knobs that you pull out, and each hand is on a different level of the keyboard. It's chaotic, but once you get the rhythm, it all works."

Damian looked up from his phone and announced,

"Our cell phone user has arrived at the Berkeley Marina. At this time of night, there's likely no one there to rent a boat to him, so I presume he'll steal one."

He continued looking at his phone and then shook his head. "He's on a boat leaving the harbor. So he's probably stealing the boat. That's another reason to get him on the island and then take the boat out of reach—I don't want to damage the boat."

"I'll let Leticia know, and then let's go down to my monitors in the lab."

Nathan nodded and then watched the four pets consume their different amounts of fish along with the dry kibble. He stayed watching them as he had a feeling that if he turned his back on Trixie, she would knock the three cats out of the way to get their food. "I'll be down as soon as they finish."

Jill followed Hermione and Damian downstairs to his lab and Nathan followed a short time later with the pets at his heels. Damian let Bella and Bailey outside, but kept Arthur inside the lab in case Jill and Nathan were able to return home that night.

The boat that Devin Vale was piloting was approaching the island. Before Jill forgot, she said to Damian, "He's got a history with explosives, so if you see him carrying a bag, find a safe place for it. I know your house can survive gunfire, but I don't know if it can survive an explosion."

Damian nodded. Their boater had researched the island and had figured out that really the only place to land was on west side unless you came with rock-climbing supplies. As the boat motored around, Damian asked Hermione, "Kiddo, are you ready to stand and defend Red Rock Island?"

"Aye, aye Captain, Sir," Hermione replied with a gleam in her eye and a salute for the upcoming battle.

"Okay, I'm taking the dinghy as it makes little noise and I'll pull that boat back quite a distance, so you'll just have the backup from Jill and Nathan for about twenty minutes."

"Seriously, Damian, I've got this."

He nodded and departed hitting the button for his fold-out dock just before he exited the lower level of the lab.

Hermione waited for the boater to get close to the island. He had bright lights turned on as he was likely looking for rocks that he wouldn't want to hit in the darkness. He stopped the boat and threw down two anchors to hold the boat in place. Then he stuck something over the hull, likely testing how deep the water was where he had stopped the boat. He disappeared for a moment and then came back out wearing what looked like waders and jumped over the side of the boat and splashed ashore. He took the waders off and left them on the beach.

The teenager was bouncing between the external cameras and the camera near the dock. She watched Damian steer a small boat around the island toward where the stolen boat lay at anchor. They watched Devin try scrambling up the cliff from the beach. The wind made enough noise to cover the sound of Damian's small motor.

"Launching drone balloons," Hermione said. "These balloons are filled with a combination of lime green dye, pepper juice, and GPS crystals. Damian patented this concoction and he's looking at a revised formula that can rest on a child's skin like a tattoo until the parents have it removed. That way, if the child is ever kidnapped, they can find them."

They watched as Damian, wearing a wet suit, quietly boarded the intruder's boat. He tied his little boat to the bigger one and checked the ignition switch for the key. He then quietly pulled up one anchor and then the other. He started the boat and put it in reverse. He hoped that the noise didn't catch the intruder's ears, but it was too late anyway, as he had backed far enough from shore that Devin couldn't swim fast enough to catch the boat. He continued to move the boat away from the island to a point where he judged Devin would die of hypothermia before he ever reached the boat by swimming in the bay. He anchored it in its new location, pocketed the key, and took his little boat back to the garage.

He entered his bottom lab area just as everyone cheered when a balloon landed squarely on the intruder's head, and from his actions, he definitely had pepper juice in his eyes. He was lying on the ground, feeling around for stuff inside the bag he'd brought with him. Damian smiled and called Leticia as he had used facial recognition earlier to identify their intruder as Devin Vale.

He gave the Coast Guard coordinates for his island and turned on all the exterior lights. He invited Jill and Nathan to follow him outside. He was carrying a water pistol filled with additional pepper spray if, for some strange reason, Devin's eyesight returned. He asked Hermione to remain inside both for her safety and to serve as backup if Devin should miraculously recover.

They walked around the man, watching him struggle, and Damian showed Jill and Nathan his lift chair from the beach. Nathan rode the chair down to bring Agent Ortiz and others up to where Devin Vale was moaning. Now that he had armed backup, Damian placed a bottle of water in Devin's hand and told him it was water to wash his eyes out. An agent with Leticia put him in handcuffs, then they debated how to get him off the island as he still couldn't see and he would fall down the path he'd climbed up. In the end, they put him in the chair with his cuffed hands zip-tied to the chair; and a Coast Guard officer waited at the bottom to cut the zip ties and get him out of the chair.

Soon he was aboard the Coast Guard cutter, and his eyes were again treated. It would be a while before the burn went away and his vision was no longer blurred. Leticia scheduled a call with them for the next day as there was a lot of evidence to collect in this case if they were to convict Devin. Much of it was computer searches from the two experts, Damian and Henrik. Damian gave the key and coordinates for the stolen boat to the Coast Guard so they could return the boat to the Berkeley Marina.

They went inside the house and found Hermione sitting on the sofa playing with her cell phone.

"Excellent job, Kiddo! How many balloons did you drop before you hit the target?"

"Just one. It helped that in the dark and with the wind noise, I could get really close to that creep. He looked up when he heard the sound, and I hit the release about two feet above his face. It was perfect. I didn't even have a chance to hit him with the water cannons. For being a real baddie, he was really easy to take down."

Nathan held out his hand out to Damian and said, "I can't thank you enough for your help with this situation. This man is a horrible human, and you and your technology took him out in such a manner that no one was hurt or even at risk. Thank you again. We'll get out of your hair, and you can have your peaceful island back if you'll give us a ride back to the marina."

Jill added, "Damian, I promised Hermione a tour of my vineyard and chemistry lab and I'd love if your whole family, including Ariana would come south so I can get your advice on how to shore up my property since I'm going to continue to try to take down the bad guys. Nathan also offered to help you build out a wine cellar here if you don't already have one or perhaps evaluate a vineyard you might want to own as that is his area of knowledge. What we're both saying is, you obviously don't need money or gifts, but we can give you our time to thank you for your help. You took on two strangers in our hour of need and helped us put away a very bad person."

"Can I drink wine when I come visit your winery? Damian and Ariana let me drink wine," Hermione asked.

"Don't believe this Kiddo for a second. We've allowed her one glass in her lifetime," Damian said with a fake frown.

"We'll follow whatever guidelines your guardians set for you," Jill said. "When I was your age, I couldn't wait to turn 21 so I could drink legally. Of course, once I could drink legally, I wondered what the big deal was: and when I was premed and then in medical school, I couldn't overindulge or I would fail. And by the time I was a practicing physician, I didn't want to do anything that might risk my license. So I guess I'm telling you that alcohol may seem like a thrill, but you'll find out in time what appeals to you and how to drink within limits."

They heard an alarm sound, "That will be Ariana. She owns the pontoon boat, which we need to get you back to the marina. I'll go help her," Hermione said, heading downstairs.

Nathan and Jill were more than ready to leave, but they wouldn't rush Damian as they were very grateful for his help.

Soon Hermione returned with Ariana and introductions were performed. She was provided with a play-by-play description of the take-down of Devin Vale.

Ariana had brought her dog, Miguel, with her as she wasn't sure if she was spending the night on the island or at her house. So Miguel met Trixie while Arthur stayed out of reach of both dogs.

Nathan and Jill decided not to mention their supplies which they were leaving in the refrigerator. Instead, they grabbed their suitcases and headed downstairs and loaded them onto the pontoon. It was nearing nine at night when they reached their car, but at least traffic wouldn't be bad on their way home. Jill hugged Damian and thanked him for his help, and they were off.

After grabbing some fast food on the way home, they pulled into the vineyard after midnight. Jill had fallen asleep on the way and was surprised when Nathan shook her awake to walk into the house.

"Maybe you should keep a score board at the side of the front door that has the score between Jill Quint and the Criminals. All the hashes would be under your name."

"I've got a lot of people helping me, so I would have to list a bunch of names after my name, but maybe if the bad guys saw the score board, they might change their minds about trying to get rid of me. I wonder how Devin was planning on killing me? He was carrying that bag and I suppose it could have contained explosives as that seems to be his thing, but I think once the FBI gets his fingerprints and DNA into the system, they might connect him to other crimes as well. As they say, this wasn't his first rodeo."

"Hopefully, you'll hear about that when you speak with Leticia in the morning. There's a lot of evidence to collect regarding him and so much of what was done to identify him was computer stuff I don't understand. They'll probably need to have Henrik and Damian assist them with that part of evidence collection."

"Henrik will look at it as just another potential sale," Jill said, and Nathan chuckled as that was indeed Henrik. "I'm so glad to sleep in our own bed tonight. I was afraid the house was going to get blown up. Thank goodness he had a delayed timer on it so the bomb squad could deactivate it and save our house."

Nathan hugged her as they walked up the stairs to the front door after making sure that Trixie took care of business before coming inside for the night.

"The evil that was Devin Vale fermented in the dark corner of the internet, but it died in the sunlight you focused on him. Dr. Quint, you're the hero in my life. Thank you for being my wife."

"Nathan, you're the hero in my life as well. You help me chase a strange occupation and protect my back when we battle the baddies. Thank you for being my partner against crime and in life. Let's go to bed."

The End

ABOUT THE AUTHOR

About the author....

I reside in Wisconsin now, though my first two dozen or so books were written while I lived in Northern California. My rescue dog and cat keep me company while I write. I love to travel, play sports, read, and drink wine and beer. I enjoy the diversity of the world and I'm always watching people and events for story ideas.

If you would like to sign up for my monthly blog and announcement of new books, please follow this link: www.alecpechebooks.com.

While you're waiting for the next story, if you would be so kind as to leave a review for this book, that would be great. I appreciate all the feedback and support. Reviews buoy my spirits and stoke the fires of creativity.

Readers that sign up for website receive a free prequel novelette for the Jill Quint Series.

<u>Jill Quint, MD Forensic Pathologist Series</u>

Time's Up (prequel short story)

Vials

Chocolate Diamonds

A Breck Death

Death On A Green

A Taxing Death

Murder At The Podium

Castle Killing

Crescent City Murder

Sicilian Murder

Opus Murder

Forensic Murder

Return to the Scene of the Crime (short story)

Embers of Murder

Ashes to Murder

Mint Death

Poisonous Murder

Sable Point Murder

<u>Damian Green Series</u>

Red Rock Island

Willow Glen Heist

The Girl From Diana Park

Evergreen Valley Murder

Long Delayed Justice

Emerald Bay Murder

Michelle Watson Series

Now You Don't See Me

Where Did She Go?

How Did She Get There?

Dog Humor

Eat, Play, Poop: Letters to my parents from camp

A. Peche

New Urban Fantasy Series - Stephanie Jones

The Awakening at Lake Tahoe (short story)

Witch's Medicine

Witch's Quest